PICKING LEMONS

A C.J. Whitmore Mystery

by

J.T. Toman

For information, email **Cozy Cat Press**,

cozycatpress@aol.com or visit our website at:

www.cozycatpress.com

COZY CAT
P R E S S

ISBN: 978-1-939816-22-1

Printed in the United States of America

Cover design by Rachel Cole

http://www.litteradesigns.com/

1 2 3 4 5 6 7 8 9 10

Acknowledgements

I am forever indebted to the economics faculty and
staff at the
University of Sydney, Yale University and Stanford
University.
Thank you for all that you taught me.

A big thank you to Patricia Rockwell for believing
in the book.

Finally, I could not have written this book without
the love and support of
Donald, Bryce and Shana. Love you!

TABLE OF CONTENTS

MONDAY

When people looked at Edmund DeBeyer, they saw the remnants of a handsome, affable man. At just over six feet with unruly, black hair and intense, blue eyes, Edmund DeBeyer had been considered the most eligible bachelor in the Ivy league when a student. The young Edmund had started a promising career in pre-med, with the idea of curing cancer or vaccinating the poor in Africa. But with a quick analysis of the hours worked to dollars earned ratio, he became an economics major instead.

On this Monday, the first day of the first week of the fall semester, Edmund DeBeyer, now a rich and renowned Eaton University economics professor, unbuttoned his tweed jacket and scanned his nine a.m. class of Econ 101 with an icy stare of distaste. Fall was his least favorite time of year. He loathed spiced pumpkin lattes, saw no beauty in dying leaves, and knew the chill in the air signaled the return of students.

This was the nation's finest? Hardly encouraging news. It appeared the future presidents, CEOs and would-be Steve Jobs's shared the IQ of a flea between them. Snippets of conversations floated unavoidably by him as the class settled into their seats.

"I just heard econ sucks majorly, dude. There's like, math, in it. We should have taken geography."

"I don't know why I'm even here. My dad gives major moolah to the school to make sure I get an A."

"What is economics exactly?"

Edmund sighed. Was this Eaton University or Elm Grove Community College?

The Chair of the department, Walter Scovill, had assigned Edmund to teach Econ 101 this fall, saying it would be "refreshing to get back to basics." Of course, it was only a coincidence that Econ 101 was everyone's least favorite course to teach, and Edmund had actively and unsuccessfully campaigned against the re-election of Walter as the Department Chair.

Really, thought Edmund. *Just like a Princeton-trained economist to be irrational and emotional.*

Princeton was, at least according to Edmund, one of the "lesser Ivies," a fact he was apt to say with a sigh of regret, just as one comments about an aged cat you know needs putting down. Edmund was touted to win the Nobel Prize in economics. Therefore, his valuable time, his $2000-per-hour consulting-rate time, was best spent on research (and consulting, of course). Not teaching a classroom of over-indulged children of semi-famous politicians over-simplified economic principles that they had no interest in learning.

Edmund sighed again. In his best, professorial monotone, he addressed the class of students whose education was the lowest priority in his life—professional or personal. He hadn't bothered to prepare a lecture for today or even pretended to glance at the textbook while walking over. The fact that each student's family was paying hundreds of dollars for every class and expecting the finest education money could buy had no impact on Edmund's attitude. The parents weren't writing the checks to him; they were writing them to Eaton, the one and same institution that had hired him as a tenured professor. So, Eaton University couldn't fire him, no matter how awful his teaching was.

"This is Econ 101. I am Professor DeBeyer. I don't care about you or who your parents are. Do not email me your excuses for poor exam grades or late assignments as I do not care if you fail. I get paid either way."

*****

At just after nine o'clock that Monday, Charles Covington III was walking down Knollwood Place, enjoying the changing leaves and the industrial-cinnamon scent that is peculiar to southern Connecticut in the fall. Knollwood Place was one of Elm Grove's more famous streets, having once been described by someone important (whose name no one could quite remember) as the most magnificent street in America. At that time, the street had been a majestic esplanade of stately nineteenth-century homes canopied with a verdant archway of elm trees. Though many of the trees had succumbed to Dutch elm disease during the intervening years and their lesser cousins, the oaks, had grown up in their place, the stately homes remained. The street, to this day, was often admired for its unique architecture and shady sidewalks. That being said, no one, important or otherwise, would have been quite so quick to bestow the "most magnificent street" title on the modern Knollwood. Ever hungry parking meters were interspersed among the trees, food trucks served try-your-luck chili to bleary-eyed, tattooed students, and, of course, Eaton University academics such as Professor Covington ambled towards their overstuffed offices that occupied the former homes of Connecticut's finest. The street had certainly lost a little of its panache.

Eighty-seven years old with a Muppet-like shock of white hair, a mustache in constant need of trimming, and two over-sized hearing aids, Charles was a distinctive figure on Eaton's campus. He favored wearing bright red suspenders, a green polka dot bow tie, dark blue trousers and a faded pink shirt stained with many past breakfasts. Charles had taught the economic history classes at Eaton University for fifty-two years and was going to teach them, *avec* red suspenders and green polka dot bow tie, until his Lord and Creator told him otherwise.

Charles's colleague, Edmund DeBeyer, found the Lord's timetable too slow for his liking. So, for the previous semester, Edmund had been gathering a petition to remove Charles Covington III from the faculty. As Edmund pointed out to the rest of the department when making his case, tenure was a career appointment, not an eternal one.

The amount of time Edmund devoted to his campaign to oust Charles was somewhat puzzling as Charles and Edmund rarely met during the course of a work day. The economics department at Eaton University was divided among four buildings. The main building, 40 Knollwood, was a cheerful red brick affair. It was here that the administrative assistant could be found, graduate classes were taught, seminars were held, and a select group of professors, with an extremely elevated view of the global interest in their research, had their offices.

The adjoining building, 42 Knollwood, was an imposing Gothic structure of grey stone. This building housed the Howard Foundation, an elite but rather dull club of microeconomists and statisticians whose existence refuted the claim of Google's chief economist that "the sexy job in the next ten years will be statisticians." It was also home to professors who were making a name for themselves but couldn't yet get office space in 40 Knollwood. Additionally and importantly for those whose research was quagmired by pedantic referees and absent coauthors, 42 Knollwood was where the faculty lounge was.

The two buildings, 40 and 42 Knollwood, were connected in the basement by the Smythe Lounge, named after John Smythe, an alumni with an abysmal GPA but an uncanny ability to invest astutely, both in the stock market and in influence. This was a place for underfunded graduate students to scrounge free coffee and the uneaten egg salad sandwiches from the previous day's catered faculty events. It was also a handy way for the faculty of 40 and 42 Knollwood to move between the two buildings without having to inconvenience themselves by going outside.

The other two economics buildings located on the opposite side of the street, 41 and 43 Knollwood, were for the "others." Such offices were assigned to professors studying the minor, less influential fields, such as economic history, development or environmental economics. One could also expect to find the professors not meeting publishing expectations on that side of the street. The dead wood, as it were. Such faculty would not only have to step outside but also cross the road if they wished to teach a class, attend a seminar, or be present at a faculty meeting. Which was a shame, given the amount of ice, snow and sleet Elm Grove experienced in any given winter.

Charles had a small office at the back of 41 Knollwood. Edmund had a resplendent suite with working fireplace and university views atop number 40. Clearly, Edmund wanted to remove his colleague from the faculty as he was troubled by the idea of Charles, not by Charles himself.

This morning, as Charles made his way to his small, cramped office, he paused and looked across the road to the main economics building, peering upwards. A frown crossed his face. "Well, that won't do," he muttered irritably. "That won't do at all." And, hooking his thumbs under his suspenders with a look of determination, Charles Covington III turned around and started to shuffle home.

*****

Jefferson Daniels, heading down from his top floor office in 40 Knollwood to the basement classroom below, was wondering what Econ 101 was thinking of its new professor. Jefferson's office was next to Edmund's, and, judging by the door-slam he heard as Edmund left to teach that morning, Jefferson did not think his treasured co-worker was embracing his new teaching assignment. Not that this was a surprise. Edmund DeBeyer was the department ego.

Jefferson should know. He and Edmund collaborated on their research, and they had done so since Jefferson was a graduate student. Though sometimes it seemed that Edmund saw the partnership not so much as a collaboration, but more as a master—errand boy arrangement. However, despite Edmund's... grandiloquent...personality, the research partnership was a net positive. Jefferson and Edmund's work in macroeconomics had been given a lot of credit for ending the recent recession and lowering the unemployment rate to a respectable level. As the hardworking Jefferson liked to say to friends outside the department, "He's the ego to my mania."

Jefferson walked into his own classroom, late as usual. He was teaching a small class of graduate students, having been much more politic over the re-election of Walter Scovill. In truth, it wouldn't have mattered how much he opposed Walter's appointment. As the only African-American faculty member in the economics department at Eaton, Jefferson was never going to get the worst teaching assignments. No Chair ever wanted to get accused of treating Jefferson like a slave.

His students were chatting amongst themselves but fell quiet when he walked in the door. After eight years of teaching, Jefferson still loved how important he felt when a room full of students fell silent because of his mere presence. *And so they should*, thought Jefferson only partly in jest. Everyone knew Jefferson's story, but no one knew it better than Jefferson himself. Grew up in the projects of New Jersey. Received his Ph.D. from Eaton University in three years, at age 22. Made a splash at UPenn as a new professor. Three years ago, aged 27, Eaton University and Professor DeBeyer lured him back to be the youngest ever tenured professor at Eaton University. Or Ee-ah-ton, as it was pronounced by Professor Daniels. Five letters. Three syllables. No chance of someone not quite catching the name.

*****

Jose Grimaldo had been trying very hard to convince the blonde, tall and alarmingly intelligent Annika Jonsdottir to form a study group with him when Professor Daniels walked in the door. Damn it.

In Jose's opinion, graduate school was like an irritating mosquito, relentlessly buzzing in his ear. Bzzz bzzz bzzz…annoying him with endless classes, problem sets and papers. And all of them about economics. But Jose was willing to pretend he liked economics in order to earn a million dollars on Wall Street when he graduated. A pretense, he suspected, that all of his classmates faked daily. Economics was way too dull for anyone to actually love it.

Jose sighed. He thought he would have had at least ten more minutes to work his magic on Annika today. Jefferson Daniels may be young and brilliant, but he was always late, infamous for spending hours in the gym or getting waylaid in corridors chatting up the secretary and students alike. What was the hurry today? It was barely ten minutes past nine.

Jose scrawled a quick note and passed it to Annika. *One thirty in the Smythe Lounge. Macro foundations and....?*

Annika read the note, blushed, and looked back at Jose. "Maybe," she whispered with a smile.

*****

Walter Scovill leaned back in his black leather desk chair, waiting for the complaints to start rolling in. It was nine-fifteen in the morning on the first day of a new semester, and faculty and students alike were going to be knocking on the door to his second floor office at 42 Knollwood Place any moment now. The only time he loathed more was exam period. How was it there were so many sick grandmothers and students with the stomach flu during the week of exams?

The reason Walter endured the hassles of being the Chair of the department (besides the obvious benefit of the $50,000 bump in pay) was that the only thing worse than listening to people complain about his decisions was not being the decision maker himself. In a department bristling with control-freaks, Walter Scovill stood above the crowd. Edmund, of course, was always challenging for the role, like a young buck eager to take over the herd.

But, of course, he is out of his league, thought Walter with a smile, imagining Edmund teaching Econ 101 at that very moment.

There were, of course, other advantages to being Department Chair. Walter exhaled deeply, thinking with satisfaction of the pretty, young, undergraduate girls with their swishing ponytails and low rise yoga pants that had been arriving on campus for the last few days. With luck, a position of power could erase 30 years, a balding head, 40 pounds of cellulite and a wedding ring. If not, expensive gifts always helped. Walter closed his eyes and relaxed into his fantasies.

Walter was jolted back to reality by a loud knock at the door. The first complainer of the day. People were so predictable.

*****

No one knew how old Betsy Williams was or how much she weighed, but those fluent in statistics considered that both numbers were high enough to make every breath she took an actuarial anomaly. Betsy was an adjunct instructor for the economics department and had been for at least thirty years. During those years, Betsy had watched junior professors come and go, students become senators, and had endured the growing egos of the tenured faculty.

Betsy had never been offered tenure. She had never asked for tenure. In fact, had anyone bothered to consider her feelings, that person would have realized she liked not being in the club of tenured professors. Betsy fully occupied her non-teaching time loving a family of one husband, five children and sixteen grandchildren that no one in the economics department had ever met or asked to meet. Betsy was so busy watching school plays and soccer games and knitting sweaters and scarves it never occurred to her to worry about who was going to win the next Nobel Prize in economics, or who was ahead in the *Journal of Political Economics* publications race in the department this year. She simply did not care.

*****

C.J. Whitmore was the first woman to be granted tenure in the economics department at Eaton University. C.J. wasn't the first female junior professor, but the first to play the tenure game successfully. She taught econometrics, the mathematics of economics, and had analyzed the data to increase the probability of getting tenure. Junior faculty of all races, genders and backgrounds worked like demons, taught their classes, published and did committee work. However, most often it was the childless, white men from the Northeast United States who were granted tenure.

C.J. didn't actually need a Ph.D. to realize the odds of her receiving tenure from an elite school steeped in New England boy's club tradition weren't in her favor. In fact, the only positive seemed to be that she was white. However, while she couldn't change her gender or where she grew up, she could make them less noticeable.

C.J. dressed in conservative suits, wore her hair tied back, and sure didn't have any kids. Hell, the only time she used the ladies' bathroom at work was after a bad shrimp taco when there was simply no choice. C.J. muted her Texas drawl and certainly made no reference to the Mom and Pop cattle ranch where she had spent her childhood. She worked 16 to 18 hours a day, only leaving her office atop 42 Knollwood for coffee hour (a.k.a. networking with the boys), and made sure her publication record was exemplary. She didn't date anyone and certainly didn't date faculty, not that she was tempted by the dried-up old meat on that smorgasbord. She taught her classes well, but not exceptionally. Everyone knew that the exceptional teachers were neglecting their research and research is king. She took the crappy committee work without complaint. And after only four years, she had tenure.

On the first day with tenure, the real C.J. arrived at work. She dressed in her hot pink cowboy boots, favorite turquoise skirt, and spangled cowgirl shirt. Her wrists clinked with bangles, and her long blonde hair swung loose. She strode into a faculty meeting and watched her colleagues' mouths hang open. "Hi, ya'll," she drawled in her natural Texas twang. "Don't let me stop you from telling your stories. You know I just love a good ball-scratcher first thing in the morning."

Walter Scovill looked as if he was going into cardiac arrest. But the tenure paperwork was signed. They were stuck with her.

The other big change C.J. made after getting tenure was she stopped going to the faculty coffee hour. "I'd prefer to be run over by a herd of buffalo," she told her friend Betsy. "At least that's over quickly. Coffee hour in the econ department? Long-winded, egotistical, old men, trying to one-up each other by talking economic balderdash. Tempting, but I'll miss."

So instead, Betsy Williams and C.J. Whitmore had coffee at Wallaby's coffee shop every morning at eleven, teaching schedules permitting. Today at coffee, C.J. was on a rant about an advertisement she had seen in *The Pug Post*, the student newspaper (whose ludicrous name only made sense if you knew the school mascot was Adorable Don the Pug). "Thirty-five thousand dollars for eggs? Have you seen the undergraduate girls? Underfed, leggy chicklets with too much makeup and not enough clothing. Would you pay thirty-five thousand dollars for any of their eggs?"

Betsy just laughed. She knew what C.J. was talking about. It wasn't uncommon for infertile couples to advertise for the eggs or sperm of Eaton students, offering large sums of money. But, you had to fit the exact description. Eaton University student, blonde, aged between 18 and 22, 4.0 GPA, fluent in four languages, and started a non-profit when you were twelve. This being Eaton, the would-be-parents were bound to find several donors who met their needs. "You're just jealous that no one wants to pay that much for your eggs," teased Betsy.

"Maybe I am. Maybe I'm just in a mood because it's the first day of semester. You know what they say. A college without students is like a picnic without ants. By the way, can you believe some idiot scheduled a seminar for today? That's as clever as putting your wedding on Super Bowl Sunday."

Betsy, sipping a large, double-whip, white-chocolate mocha, clucked comfortingly. She didn't have to go to seminars, being an adjunct instructor. In fact, she would be teaching in the afternoon.

"And, it isn't just any old seminar. Edmund the Ego is giving it. I wonder if he even realizes that half the department is still on vacation, and the rest will be writing their syllabi while he drones on. And he's lecturing us on solving unemployment. How about I just liven things up and point out that a group of doughy, old men with tenured jobs wouldn't understand the first thing about being unemployed?"

Betsy nodded and clucked some more. She had never understood the point of the "seminar," even when she was an eager young graduate student here at Eaton University. In theory, it was supposed to be a collegial sharing of knowledge, with your fellow academics offering helpful suggestions and ideas. But Betsy had always felt it was akin to the Roman Coliseum. The presenter was the prey, and the audience tried to kill him or her by picking apart the paper one pedantic, self-promoting comment at a time.

C.J. was still talking, and Betsy tuned back in. "Talking about unemployment, has the endowment at Eaton University shrunk so much we had to fire the maintenance staff?"

Betsy stared at C.J. in astonishment. "What are you talking about?"

"I looked out my window this morning and saw Charles Covington, octogenarian professor, carrying a ladder towards the department. It must have been about ten a.m., give or take. This is America, the land of the 'free to hire as much low-paid immigrant help as we need.' The Lord Almighty would expect Noah to use sub-contractors to build the Ark. What the hell is the man up to?"

*****

Mary Beth Sanders couldn't stop admiring her new manicure. The fall leaves were darling, and the shade of red was awesome. With a capital O. Or was than an A? Whatever. There were so many freaking letters in the alphabet. How was one to keep track?

The best thing about her job as an administrative assistant at Eaton University was how close she was to New York City. No skanky, Elm Grove beauty school intern was touching her nails. It wasn't worth the risk.

Mary Beth wasn't going to be an assistant forever. No way. By the time she was twenty-five, at the very, very oldest, she was going to be a wife. A rich man's wife. Mary Beth was attractive…five feet, seven inches, slender, with long brunette hair. But Mary Beth understood that attractive women are like rats. They are on every street corner of every continent, and one looks just like another. No, to become a rich man's wife, attractive wasn't going to cut it. You needed to be... exquisite. So exquisite that all the rats would run away, and the rich husband would just see you. The manis, pedis, Brazilians, tints, microderms and Vicki Secrets spending sprees were all an investment. Ensuring her exquisiteness and therefore Mr. Rich. You didn't need an economics degree to understand that.

In the meantime, she had to tend to this administrative dribble. Would lunchtime never come? God, the big hand had to move from the nine to the twelve on her watch before it was time to eat. What was that? Another, um, ten…no…fifteen minutes. That was like, hours.

Why couldn't these professors do their own work? They treated her like a slave, and slavery ended, you know, like years ago. Take Edmund DeBeyer. Apparently he couldn't even type his own letters. Mary Beth put in the Dictaphone headphones and started to transcribe.

"Dear Professor Brustad,"

Mary Beth paused. Professor. Was that one F and two S's. Or two F's and one S? What was that saying her friend told her? Oh yeah. *F*un is *S*hoe *S*hopping. One F, two S's.

Mary Beth resumed typing.

"Thank you for your letter. I am honored by your positive recommendation.

In regards to your question of the jointly authored work, I have always liked to assist the careers of graduate students and young faculty by allowing them to be included as co-authors on papers where they have assisted me as research assistants.

Regards,
Professor Edmund DeBeyer"

Mary Beth was just finishing her typing, correcting "reccomendation" to "recommendation," "asisst" to "assist," and "carreers" to "careers," after spell check alerted her to the mistakes, when she heard a voice whisper behind her, "I love your nails. Did you get them done for me?"

Twirling around in her office chair, she saw Jefferson Daniels leaning against the wall. Professor Daniels was her current number one pick as Mr. Rich Husband. Smiling coquettishly, Mary Beth uncrossed and re-crossed her long legs, pausing just long enough during the process for Jefferson to catch a glimpse of what could be his. "Of course I did. Now, what else can I do for you today, Professor?"

*****

Stephen Choi stared angrily at his watch, trying to change the time with his death glare. Two o'seven. Late for seminar. Why did he care? He had been a junior faculty member at Eaton for six years, relegated to 43 Knollwood, and, despite some excellent publications, had just had his request for tenure denied. Now, he had just one year to find another job or join the unemployment lines. He could give this seminar on unemployment in two words. It sucked.

According to the vicious departmental gossip vine, Edmund DeBeyer headed the faction that argued against his appointment. DeBeyer didn't want yet another trade economist in the department. *"I think we need to practice some trade and exchange some trade economists for something a little more cutting edge. We can sweeten the deal with a development person if needed."* Edmund DeBeyer did not believe that all economists were created equal.

Stephen tried to sneak into the back of the basement seminar room in 40 Knollwood, hoping no one would notice he was a few minutes late. However, to his surprise, the seminar room contained only three people, and the seminar hadn't started. This couldn't be good. Edmund was notoriously punctual and expected the rest of the faculty to be waiting eagerly, grateful to learn from the master.

Stephen slipped into the seat next to C.J. "Where is our Lord and master? And, for that matter, most of his kingdom?"

C.J., who had been aimlessly scrolling through her Facebook page on her smart phone, looked up at her colleague. "Stephen, honey, you want to watch your tongue. You know Edmund leases heaven to God. He can have you struck by lightning any time he likes."

"No, really. What's going on?"

"Well, Edmund underestimated the faculty's ability to relax, and, clearly, many of your colleagues have chosen to spend an additional day in Maui. As for Professor DeBeyer himself, he's just running late. Jeffy, darling, has toodled up to his office to tell him we are waiting. Now just sit your patootie down in that chair and talk to me. I want to hear what your plans are. There is life after Eaton you know and, most definitely, a very nice life."

Stephen scowled. His look said, "You are so wrong. The rest of the world is just an empty wasteland." C.J. smiled and was about to joke that Harvard was probably as dire as his look indicated, but he shouldn't write off Stanford, when Jefferson burst into the room.

"I need help. Please, someone call 9-1-1. Something is wrong with Edmund. I think…I think…he's dead!"

TUESDAY

The next day, Tuesday, started with *The Pug Post* running the eye catching, if rather unimaginative, headline "PROFESSOR MURDERED!" All across campus, students emerged from their dorms rooms deprived of both sleep and the ability to dress in warm, functional clothing. As the day was, somewhat predictably for Elm Grove at the beginning of fall, cool and breezy, the scantily clad students spent the day huddled in shivering groups, reading *The Pug* and speculating on who the killer was. The five thousand undergraduate students at Eaton University, being of an age and social class which naturally lent them to a me-focused view of the world, were sure they knew the killer personally, swore they were the intended victim (saved only by cutting class that day), and were very thankful the murder increased the Goth-cool image of Eaton. The preppies at Harvard were going to be weeping into their polo shirts that night.

While questionably the most magnificent street in America, Knollwood Place was now, without doubt, the most popular. Television vans, with their satellite dishes perched on top like flowers on a preacher's wife's hat, jockeyed for parking spaces. On-the-spot correspondents breathlessly reported back dramatic twenty-second accounts of the action, padding their two seconds of news ("he's dead") by making serious faces and commenting on the sadness of the day. Students and townsfolk crowded along the street, taking photos of the building "where it happened!!" for their

Facebook and Tumblr pages and sending ghoulish tweets such as "at 40 Knollwood. footsteps behind me. ahhhhh" or "Top reason to drop econ: Its murderously hard! LOL!" Frustrated, the Elm Grove police department had to post multiple officers for crowd control. The Chief refrained from saying that in a city with as much drug and gun crime as Elm Grove, one measly professor was hardly worth this much man-power. Experience taught him that the interest would be short-lived.

*****

At nine o'clock that morning, C.J., having battled her way through the crowds and made it very clear to several insistent reporters that they would get more information from a headless, rotisserie chicken, stood in the doorway of her graduate, upper-level econometrics class. Sadly, she counted only seven students. If you asked C.J., every graduate student should be an econometrics major. Without statistics and data, her colleagues' theories about unemployment or trade or the plight of those poor Starbucks-less countries were just ideas, fantasy novels, really. Surely, the brightest minds of tomorrow would want the skills to unlock the planet-saving information that people were telling economists every time they went to the store or didn't go, as the case may be. C.J. counted again. Seven. The data indicated the graduate students thought otherwise.

No surprise; all the chatter currently in her classroom was about Edmund DeBeyer and his untimely demise.

"Do you think one of the professors did it?"

"Of course. The only surprise is that it didn't happen sooner."

"I'm starting a betting pool. Every faculty member is a contender. Five bucks to enter. Winner takes all."

"I'm in!"

"I'll take two names. Double the odds. Who says I'm not a statistical genius."

"Hey, do you think the murderer will kill one of us?"

"Yeah. You're just as important and irritating as Professor DeBeyer. In fact, I used to get the two of you confused."

"Dick."

"That's Dr. Dick to you."

"Not for at least another eight years, my friend."

As C.J. walked to the front of the class, her students fell silent, and Jose, the self-appointed leader of the graduate cohort, raised his hand.

"Yes, Jose?" asked C.J. "You have a question?"

"How 'bout we investigate who did it, Professor Whitmore? You know, use our stats skills on a real problem for once."

C.J. could see from the nods and smiles of his classmates, this plan had the support of the entire group. They wanted something more exciting than solving the widget production problems for Factory X. C.J., while not a big fan of widgets, was not easily swayed by the whims of her students. "Jose, this is a class on advanced econometrics, not *CSI: Summer Camp.*"

Jose had not made it from working as a rent boy in Tijuana to a promising graduate student at one of the nation's most selective universities because he took no for an answer. With his Latin good looks and impish smile, he made his way in this world using charm and persistence and, if necessary, bargaining and lying. Even his graduate school application, actually his third application (this time as "Jose"), had been 25% truth, 25% interpretation and 50% creative writing.

"Professor Whitmore," Jose placated, using the tone of an experienced mediator who knew how to soothe two warring spouses into an amicable agreement, "what would be the harm? Part of Eaton's mission statement is to create knowledge. I think you and I and the rest of the class could do that here, by applying the invaluable statistical knowledge that you are going to impart to us."

C.J. narrowed her eyes and looked at Jose closely. There was something about that boy. He reminded her of a horse she once owned. Fast and talented, but would buck unexpectedly. She tapped her index finger to her chin as she thought about his proposal. For all she knew, one of the students sitting in her class was the killer. Goodness knew, Edmund had annoyed enough of them. She could still remember finding Annika sniffling in the Smythe Lounge at the end of last spring.

"I go see him, to show him my thesis work," sniffed *Annika.*

C.J. had nodded, not understanding the problem. Annika's work was very good.

"He says to me, 'What are you doing here? My undergraduate office hours are tomorrow at seven am.'"

Annika had burst into a fresh round of tears, remembering.

"I am his Ph.D. student! I have been working for him for two years. He does not even recognize me!"

C.J. turned and addressed the whole class. All seven of them. "If we wanted to create a model to find a murderer, what is our biggest problem?"

Jose answered quickly, with an air of ghoulish enjoyment, "He finds out and kills us all."

The class giggled, enjoying themselves. The start of advanced econometrics was turning out to be much more exciting than they had hoped.

C.J. sighed heavily. "That is actually not too far from the truth and is my biggest concern. But, as we are supposed to be a room of economists, or almost-economists, I was speaking economically. So, what economic problem does this case remind us of?"

As if turning a switch, the giggling stopped and a deathly silence filled the room. The students shifted uncomfortably in their seats, hoping one of their classmates knew the answer.

C.J. waited them out. This was their idea. These students were in at least their second year of the doctoral program, for some, many more. They should be able to come up with one idea among them.

The seconds dragged painfully by.

C.J. sat on the edge of her desk, swung her pink cowboy boots and whistled. "Feel free to consult any notes or textbooks," she commented with an air of feigned casualness that did not mask her impatience.

There were sounds of shuffling, pencils being chewed on, and chairs squeaking across the floor as the students vainly searched for the answer.

Finally, Annika raised a tentative hand. "Is this...is this like the market for second-hand cars?" she asked uncertainly. "But, instead of trying to pick out the bad car from the good ones when we are shopping for a used car, we are trying to pick out the guilty person from the innocent people?"

"Honey," said C.J. with genuine enthusiasm, "you're like a ray of sunshine in a dank and muddy pigsty. Yes. Your used car dealer has a bad car, a lemon as it were, but has polished it real nice, maybe even turned back that odometer. It is, therefore, hard to know which is a good car and which is a bad car. Same here. The murderer is going to try and present himself as an innocent person, making it hard to tell who just didn't like Professor DeBeyer," C.J. paused and looked pointedly at her students, causing them to giggle self-consciously, "and who is a killer."

Annika beamed, and Professor Whitmore turned her attention to Jose. "If you want to model this, young man, to 'create knowledge' as you say, you want to be able to pick the lemon. Capiche?"

Jose nodded.

"Now, enough with that. Let's turn our attention to the real topic for today."

As C.J. turned to the blackboard, ready to start class, she heard Annika whisper to Jose.

"Don't you have anything to say to me? Like where you were at one-thirty yesterday? I ended up missing the seminar, not that it mattered."

"Sorry," Jose whispered back meekly. "I forgot that I was late in paying some of my student fees. I had to take care of it right away."

That's odd, thought C.J. *I thought Jose was on full scholarship.*

*****

"Well, if this doesn't blow the flies off your dung pile, I don't know what does," drawled C.J. as Betsy approached her in Wallaby's coffee shop two hours later.

Betsy noticed that C.J., coffee in hand, had opted against the traditional mourning color of black and was instead decked out in red, skin-tight, velvet jeans, a yellow shirt that jangled as she moved, and the ever-present hot pink cowboy boots. Grief, Texas-style. Betsy, wearing a dark grey dress and low-heeled black shoes, lowered herself down into a comfortable couch seat with an audible sigh and pulled out her ever-present knitting.

"Well, I watch enough *Law and Order*," said Betsy, in response to C.J.'s suggestion that she should be surprised by Edmund's death. "Those gruesome deaths are supposed to be true stories, 'ripped from the headlines' they say. So, I guess I shouldn't be shocked that something like that could happen here." Betsy paused for a moment. "Do you think they'll make a *Law and Order* episode about this murder?"

"Um, sure. I guess they could," C.J. hazarded an answer to Betsy's question.

"I knew it!" cried Betsy. "I said so to Mr. Williams when I heard the news. I said, 'Mark my words, honey. Edmund's death is weird enough to be a *Law and Order*.' How wonderful. Now, tell me all the details of yesterday, so I can recognize the episode when I see it."

C.J. smiled to herself. More evidence that traditional economic theorists like Walter Scovill needed to rethink their research. Walter, like most economists, based his research on a set of assumptions, a favorite being that people are rational.

Rational people are devoid of emotion, but simply make the best choice for themselves every time, having considered all the available information. They never impulse buy apps for their smart phone or overeat nachos while watching *Monday Night Football* or procrastinate about saving money. C.J. had looked closely, but she had never found a rational person. And it didn't look like she was going to stumble on one today. The woman sitting opposite her had just described a murder as "wonderful" because it might be made into an episode of her favorite TV show. Surprising? No. Rational? Well...

C.J. took a long sip of coffee and then looked up, ready to answer Betsy's request for details. "Well, we gathered yesterday at two o'clock for Edmund's hideously boring seminar. But, notably, not everyone was there. In fact, to begin, there was only myself, Peter Johansson, that Industrial Organization economist over in 43 Knollwood, and Walter. Annika and Jose, Edmund's Ph.D. students, didn't show, which I suspect had something to do with a lover's tiff. Charles never showed, but that isn't a big surprise. He was probably at home getting an early start on his 'fivesies.' Jefferson scraped it in right at two o'clock, panting like a Labrador in July. Clearly he had been on another one of those painful-looking runs. I'm all for being outdoors, but you know, I've never seen a cow or a sheep run laps around a pasture for 'fun.' People are just plain weird. You ever see a horse strap a parachute to its back and jump out of an airplane? And people say that animals are dumb. Uh huh. And Stephen showed up, but late. My guess is he was in his office performing ancient Chinese death rituals against Edmund for leading the charge against his tenure."

Betsy looked up from her knitting, with the alertness of a hound sniffing the scent. "Sure looked like those death rituals worked. Are you sure that's all Stephen was doing?"

C.J. frowned. Hell, yes, she was sure, wasn't she? This was Stephen, the runt of the faculty litter. "Betsy, this isn't actually *Law and Order*. We're talking about Stephen. The man can't tie his own shoelaces without falling over. How is he going to strangle Edmund with a Harvard Ph.D. hood?"

Betsy shuddered, gleefully. "Is that really how he died? Strangled with his beloved Harvard hood? You know, Edmund loved to wear his academic robes around the office. He said they made him think professorial thoughts."

"Yep. Well, he wore them one too many times. While he was standing at the whiteboard in his office, someone came up from behind and..." C.J. made the motion of tightening a knot with her hands.

Betsy put her hands up to her face, half in horror, half in delight. This story was going to carry her through many a bake sale, school play and piano recital. No one she knew had anything nearly as exciting to tell.

Without doubt, as someone who knew a murdered man, she was going to be the center of attention in the Elm Grove Grandma Brigade for a long, long time. Betsy refocused her gaze on C.J., waiting for more sordid yet splendid details.

"Back to yesterday," C.J. continued. "Walter, Peter, Jeffy and I were sitting around in the seminar room, waiting for Edmund, and, of course, all four of us were seriously annoyed at both the incredible waste of time and having to waste it with each other. We were all desperately faking interest in our cell phones, so we didn't have to talk to each other. At about five after two, when Edmund still hadn't shown, Jeffy offered to look for him and toodled off. Stephen arrived a few minutes later, grumpy at the world. Then, Jeffy returned shortly after that and gasped that Edmund was dead."

C.J. paused and took a sip of her coffee.

"Oh, for the love of Our Lord. Don't stop there. Then what happened?" asked Betsy.

"Well, at first, we thought God was sick of being Edmund's number two and had struck the man down with a heart attack or the like. So Walter called 9-1-1, and I said that I knew CPR, which is true-ish. I know how to do CPR on a cow. So I ran down to Edmund's office with Jeffy and that's when I saw that no amount of CPR was going to make that seminar happen."

Betsy had the decency to look a little green and briefly slowed her knitting. "You actually saw him? All strangulated, lying in his office?"

"You bet your knitting needles I did. The police reckon he had been killed sometime in the hour before we found him, so it was okay. He was freshly dead, like a pig at a spit roast. Not smelly, maggoty dead, which would have been terrible."

"Oooooh," said Betsy, deliciously horrified and wishing she had a pen and paper to write down the details before she forgot them. She was forgetting more and more these days. Mr. Williams teased her and said she was going to forget him one of these days. Like that would ever happen. After fifty-four years of marriage, Betsy could recognize her husband's belch at a beer and brats BBQ. "Did you see anything else important while you were there? Like muddy footprints, or cigarette butts?"

"Sadly, I think everyone else also watches *Law and Order* and so are pretty careful with the evidence they leave behind at a murder scene," commented C.J. dryly. "As the police don't think a stranger did it, I don't think fingerprints are going to narrow it down. The fingerprints of every faculty member and student going back three hundred years are in that office. The only thing that was strange was a ladder outside Edmund's window, but I think it belonged to Charles. Remember, I saw him with one earlier in the day."

"Disappointing," sighed Betsy. "It's unlikely Charles did it. He's almost ninety. If he had a beef with Edmund, he could have taken care of it years ago, when he had the strength. But what do you mean, the police don't think a stranger did it? Do they think…one of the faculty did? Or a student?"

"So I gather," said C.J. "I guess burglars have a tendency to steal things and nothing was taken. And the method of killing was very…personal. We all got to spend a long time last night answering the same question. Basically, where were we in the hours leading up to two o'clock yesterday afternoon?"

"And where was everyone?"

"To be honest, I can't say for sure. They asked us individually. But, of course, we all chatted afterwards. Jefferson was indignant on Edmund's behalf that so few faculty had shown up for the seminar. I didn't like to point out that the real issue wasn't how many people turned up to Edmund's seminar, but rather the fact someone didn't let him live to present it."

"Well, do you know where the rest of the faculty were?" asked Betsy.

"Well, quite a few people in 40 and 42 Knollwood have sabbatical this semester, so they were understandably absent as they are visiting other colleges. But the majority of the faculty didn't make the seminar because they were either at home or out of town, extending the summer vacation. You know who I mean. It must have been a ghost town at 41 and 43 Knollwood."

Betsy just murmured. She was always amazed by the bitchiness in an academic department.

"For those of us who were around, from best I can tell," continued C.J., "Edmund went to the faculty lounge for coffee at eleven, as per usual. Both Jefferson and Stephen saw him there. Why Stephen was at faculty coffee is anyone's guess. Sucking up now is not going to help. The tenure decision was final. Oh, Peter Johansson, he was there too. Anyway, Stephen says he left about eleven-thirty and went back to his office and was there doing research and job hunting until he caught sight of the clock and ran to seminar. Jefferson and Edmund left the lounge together at eleven-forty-five, and Peter was still there when they left. Peter must have left right after though, as he was teaching a graduate seminar from noon until one-fifty. Edmund went to his office and told Jefferson he planned to spend the afternoon there until the seminar. Jefferson says he went back to his office, changed and went on his usual two hour run, but you can bet a silver dollar he detoured via Mary Beth's desk on the way."

Betsy nodded. "Well, that seems to fit in with what we know, anyhow. You said Stephen came in late, and

Jefferson came in right on time, clearly straight from a workout."

"Right," said C.J. "Those two seem to check out. Charles wasn't in his office when the police did a door check to make sure no one else had been killed, so I guess he spent the afternoon at home. Walter was teaching from ten-thirty until eleven-fifty and then had a lunch meeting at that pho place..."

Betsy interrupted. "Walter had lunch at a pho place? Huh. I didn't think he was a noodle soup kind of guy."

"He's not. He was lunching with the Chair of the Business School, who was just back from Vietnam and very keen to relive the culinary experience. Walter suffered through it from noon until one. I can only guess he really wants something from the Chair of the Business School. Walter was then in his office until the seminar. I, of course, met you for coffee here at eleven and then sat outside on Knollwood collecting parking meter data until the seminar started."

Betsy looked troubled. "No one seems to have a really solid alibi for the time of the murder. Stephen was alone in his office, as was Walter. I think you are right about Charles. He probably went home for lunch and didn't come back. Jefferson was out running. Even you, you were sitting outside with parking meters. I bet no one saw you the whole time. If people were teaching or out of town or at home with their family, that's okay. But otherwise..." Betsy petered out.

"What can they expect? That is what academics do all day. Sit by themselves and think. Or run by themselves and think, in the case of Jefferson."

Betsy paused to think for a moment, though she was once again knitting at a blinding pace. Today was a bright red and blue sweater with a sail-boat on the front for a seven-year-old grandson. "They say the most common killer is the spouse. Has anyone thought about Lisa?"

C.J. just snorted. "I'm sure the police have. If it were Walter who was killed, Mrs. Scovill would be high on my list. Imagine living with Walter, listening to him drone on about his theories on the marginal benefits of sexual relations, factoring in, of course, the length of a marriage and the attractiveness index of each spouse. It's amazing the man is still alive."

Betsy tried to stifle a laugh. Sometimes C.J. was just too...honest.

"But Lisa," continued C.J., "she didn't even have to live with Edmund. That woman is safely tucked away in New York City with her art gallery. Amazing as it is to think of Edmund being married, those two were perfect for each other. Each is so self-absorbed, they didn't notice the other one wasn't there. There's no reason for her to kill Edmund. They barely saw each other as it was.

"I do have something funny to tell you though," C.J. said, seamlessly changing the topic, without apparently taking a breath. "My graduate class thought they were going to investigate the crime, as a case study. Jose, of course, was leading the charge. Citing the 'Mission of Eaton University' as the reason I should let this farce occur in my classroom."

Betsy looked at her, suddenly worried. "You aren't going to let them, are you? I know it would be so interesting. Like that fellow on that show, *Numbers*. He always finds the murderer using mathematical models. Like you say, the data hold the answers. It's just a case of knowing how to let it speak. But I don't think it's a good idea for the students. It might not be safe."

"No, no. The students aren't doing anything," reassured C.J. "But Annika did notice this is just like the market for used cars. As a buyer, you don't know which cars are good and which are bad. So the owners of the lemons try to off-load them by making their cars look good, and the owners of the good cars need to let you know their cars are actually the real deal, so they can sell them. You know, with warranties, test drives, return policies and the like. The murder market can't be any different. The innocent will want to let the police and the rest of the world know they didn't do this, so they don't go to jail. Come forth with their alibis and a lack of motive and so on. And the murderer..."

"Won't the murderer try to disguise himself as a 'good car,' so to speak?" asked Betsy. "How will you tell the difference?"

"I guess that is the $64,000 question. How do you pick the lemon?"

*****

Tuesday, the first Edmund-free day of Walter Scovill's life, was not beginning as he had imagined it would. He had fantasized countless times about a life without the egocentric, pompous jackass whose astonishing similarity to Walter was what annoyed him the most. Without the irritation of Edmund, Walter always pictured an idyllic life, awash in accolades and glory. But this morning there were no marching marionette bands, proclaiming Walter to be the Greatest Economist That Ever Lived. Missing also were the people lining the streets, cheering his name. And, sadly, he was not having warm, scented oil rubbed over his fleshy, naked body by a nimble fingered, obliging Asian masseuse. Instead, before he even had an opportunity to pay an underemployed, art history major to make his first cup of shade-grown, hand-picked, baptized-with-sun-warmed-water coffee, Walter was being questioned by the police. Again.

"Where was he between 1:00 p.m. and 2:00 p.m. on the day in question?"

Walter sighed. Being questioned by the police was not like a fine wine. It certainly didn't improve over time. How often would he have to answer this question? He was in his office. Alone. So, yes, he realized there wasn't anyone who could corroborate it. That was one of the defining characteristics of being alone. There was no one else there.

Then, just before two o'clock, he was walking through the Smythe Lounge to the seminar room. Then, he was sitting in the seminar room. This was not rocket science. Walter wondered what the average IQ of a policeman was. Certainly not high enough to form a MENSA membership voting bloc. An average IQ of 85 maybe? Perhaps 85 was the national average, skewed upwards by some bright stars. The ones that all those T.V. shows seemed to be based on. The average of the Elm Grove police force seemed closer to 70.

"What happened at the seminar?"

Walter shook his head in disbelief. Really, did he have to write the questions for these imbeciles? They weren't going to get any information at this rate. Nothing happened at the seminar as the seminar did not take place owing to the fact the presenter was murdered.

"I think what you meant to ask was what happened in the seminar *room* leading up to the discovery of Edmund's body," Walter corrected pedantically.

And nothing unusual happened, except that Edmund had expected all the faculty to be assembled for his seminar and only five people showed. Walter himself wasn't surprised by the turnout. It was the first day of semester, which did not equate to the first day of work for a lot of professors. One of the benefits of a Ph.D. is you get a lot of flex time.

But it would have been a blow to Edmund. Typically, faculty only attend seminars in their field areas. But Edmund was a very distinguished faculty member. He demanded a certain level of...attention... as he was highly favored to get the Nobel Prize this year. Sadly, for Eaton University and its publicity machine, that could no longer happen. As Walter was sure the police knew, you must be living to receive the Nobel.

Walter paused in his musings. There was one faculty member who had been at work, who wasn't at the seminar. Charles Covington III was not in attendance. But that was not a surprise either. Charles was almost ninety years old and was a little...old. Walter was not willing to say out loud, even to a pair of imbecilic Elm Grove policemen, that the renowned economics department of Eaton University had a senile member of staff.

"Anyway, in the seminar *room* at two o'clock," Walter emphasized with an overbearing condescension, "there were four professors waiting for Edmund. Myself, Jefferson Daniels, Peter Johansson and C.J. Whitmore. After about five minutes, the troops got restless, and Jefferson volunteered to look for him. No surprise there. Edmund and Jefferson work together. The paper being presented was half Jefferson's work. At least half, I would say. Anyway, while Jefferson was away, Stephen Choi tried to sneak into the room like a naughty child. Please. As if we care. We've already denied his tenure. And then Jefferson came back at about ten after the hour and told us Edmund was dead."

"Had you scheduled any maintenance work for the building that day?"

Walter shook his head and cursed inwardly. That damn ladder. What was the deal with that damn ladder?

"No," Walter replied dryly. "There should not have been a ladder outside Edmund's window."

"Isn't that a rather strange place for a ladder?"

Walter looked blankly at the policemen in front of him. "You mean, up against a wall, serving its intended purpose of allowing people to easily ascend walls?" Walter said icily. "No, I cannot agree. I don't think it is all that strange for a ladder to be leaning against a wall. Perhaps, instead, you want to find who was using it for its intended purpose. A gang member? A burglar? This is Elm Grove after all. Rated the fourteenth most dangerous city in America. Not a statistic that Eaton University puts in its glossy brochures."

The police seemed nonplussed by his suggestion. Apparently Elm Grove's street element strongly favored guns. There wasn't a single gang known to crime enforcement at the moment that used strangling via academic gown as their method of killing. And as for burglars, characteristically they stole things. The fact that nothing was missing from Edmund's office strongly pointed away from Walter's burglar theory. Walter couldn't help but agree. You didn't have to be Einstein to work this out. He knew the stranger theory was a long shot, but a more comforting idea than the alternative. That one of them...a Pug...

"Was there a member of your faculty who disliked Edmund DeBeyer?"

Walter snorted with laughter at the two policemen sitting on the other side of his desk. They hadn't worked this out already? He was lowering their IQ estimate to 60.

No. There was not "a member" of the faculty who disliked Edmund DeBeyer. However, there was "a faculty" that disliked Edmund DeBeyer. The closest thing he had to a friend was Jefferson Daniels. As he said before, they worked together.

"How much did the faculty dislike Edmund DeBeyer?"

Walter paused, trying to select an Edmund story that would make the situation clear.

"Five years ago," began Walter, "before Jefferson joined the faculty, Edmund ran for the position of Chair of the department unopposed. I was on sabbatical, in case you were wondering. Even without an opponent, Edmund lost. The by-laws state you have to get a vote to be appointed, and Edmund DeBeyer didn't get a single one."

Walter could see the policemen had many more questions, but he escorted them rather impolitely out of his office. He did not have the time or inclination to provide the answers.

Walter had been summoned to the office of the President of the University. Under any circumstances, Walter Scovill did not enjoy the company of men with more power than he. When he was on the defensive, it was intolerable.

*****

Stephen Choi spent the morning pacing back and forth in his small cupboard of an office. He was so confused. Yesterday was so confusing. He thought it would make everything better, but it had just muddled things in his brain. His friends had told him "confront your nemesis" and "face your troubles head on," but it hadn't worked out as he thought it would. Now he simply didn't know what to do.

Perhaps he should leave. Disappear. But that didn't seem right somehow. He was sure running away would be frowned upon. What if he left a letter? Explaining everything. Then he could leave with a clear conscience. Better, but still...an apology. Multiple apologies. To everyone in the department. Stephen was beginning to feel like he had struck on a plan. That would atone for his actions. Then he could go.

*****

The President's secretary gave Walter a pitying look. Her phone buzzed and she said "You can go in now, Professor Scovill." Her look said, "You poor, poor thing."

Walter squared his shoulders. He had nothing to apologize for. A colleague had unfortunately been killed. It was a tragedy. He could talk to the President about it, man to man.

Walter opened the heavy oak door of the President's office and saw not one man, but three. Sitting in the office was the President, the Provost and the Dean of Arts and Sciences.

"Walt! Take a seat!" boomed the President.

Walter sat on the edge of a leather armchair. He hated being called Walt. Especially by someone he knew about as well as an airline ticketing agent on the phone in Bangalore. He grimaced at the President, trying to exude the required air of collegiality that he was incapable of feeling. To be fair, none of the other men in the room were invested in collaboration or team-building either, but they had perfected the art of faking it, hence their rise to prominent administrative positions within the college.

This meeting had been called for one reason and one reason only. The death of Edmund DeBeyer had upset the administrative equilibrium at Eaton University, and all three men waiting for Walter were determined to ensure it was set right. The questions and instructions began to ricochet around the room.

The Dean wanted to know Walter's plan for having someone teach Edmund's class for the rest of semester. "And what form of counseling are you offering the faculty and students, Walter? It is so important to be seen as caring, even if the therapy is crap. Get therapy dogs in for all I care. They look great on camera and everyone loves a dog-healing story."

The Provost was concerned about the impact on student recruitment and the faculty hiring they had planned in January. "What are your plans to overcome these issues, Walter? We need to get in a replacement for Edmund ASAP. Someone equally as notable and likely to win the Nobel. Harvard is ahead in the count, you know."

The President didn't want there to be any negative impact on fundraising, or students being withdrawn by overly-concerned parents. "Now, Walt, how are we going to ensure this little incident that you have let happen doesn't affect the bottom line for the university? Think of the endowment, son. Harvard's still up on us by $10 billion, and, by God, I plan to overtake them during my reign."

Walter smiled, nodded, and murmured such phrases as "I'll work up a plan" and "I'll send you a memo" and "I'm so glad you asked." All the time thinking "How can it be that you get paid five times more than I do?"

*****

Mary Beth went down to New York after the police allowed her to leave the office the previous night to have a special "mourning mani" done on her nails. Gone was the cheerful red of autumn. Now she was displaying a jet black, with Professor DeBeyer's initials (P.D.) in electric pink on each nail surrounded by a heart of white tears.

Paired with her outfit of black, knee high, shiny, vinyl boots and a Ross Dress for Less, Imitation-Designer, black mini, Mary Beth felt that today was the day that her efforts would comfort Professor Daniels into a marriage proposal.

True to form, Jefferson stopped by just before eleven, protein shake in hand, on his way to coffee time in the faculty lounge. While Jefferson Daniels made nice with his colleagues (and their influence in getting grant money) during coffee time, caffeine never polluted his body. The rest of the faculty was happy to wash down Dunkin' Donuts with Mary Beth's finest brew. But Jefferson only drank protein shakes, herbal teas or wheatgrass smoothies.

"Oh, Professor," Mary Beth gushed, "I am so, so, so sorry. Such a dear friend. Such a great man."

Jefferson bowed his head in acknowledgement. "Thanks, Mary Beth," he said somberly.

"And it's not like he just died, natural like. He was murdered. And we don't know by who. Maybe, like, one of us. It's so creepy."

Jefferson looked pained, but it wasn't clear if that was from grief or Mary Beth. He patted her hand. "I'm sure it was just an Elm Grove gang thug. No one we knew or that will bother us again."

"The police don't seem to think so. I guess Edmund wasn't really a gang type. Though he could be kinda mean sometimes."

Jefferson, not his usual flirty self, was moving away from Mary Beth's desk.

"Were you questioned by the police?" asked Mary Beth, desperate to keep Jefferson a few minutes longer. "I was. They were, like, so interested. I told them that I took my lunch at noon, as usual. I walked down to Bruegger's Bagels and took the latest Stephanie Plum novel with me. I just love those books. Maybe I should be a bounty hunter. What do you think?"

Jefferson looked like he thought he had spent too much time listening to Mary Beth.

Unaware that reliving the events of yesterday was not the best way to console the man, Mary Beth continued recounting her tales with the police. "I told them that, just as I was finishing lunch, I saw Stephen walking towards downtown. I was sitting in Bruegger's at, like just before one. He looked so darn secretive I reckon he has a paid 'lunch date' at the Motel 6. I mean, the man has been here six years, and we've never seen a girlfriend. It's unnatural to go that long without some nooky."

Jefferson interrupted the girl, suddenly interested. "What did you say about Stephen?"

"I saw him yesterday, going downtown, at about one o'clock."

"And you told this to the police?"

"Of course. Why?"

"No reason," said Jefferson, thinking back to Stephen telling everyone he was in his office yesterday at one. "Please. Carry on." He smiled an encouraging smile at Mary Beth.

Giggling, Mary Beth continued. "Well, then I went back to my desk, as my lunch ends at one, you know. I can see, like, so much from my desk, as the window looks out onto the street, and I can see out the door too. I don't think people realize. I saw C.J. sitting outside in a lawn chair from, like, noon, when I left for lunch, until two. I mean, I didn't see her the whole time, because I was off eating lunch for some of it. But she kept getting up and writing down stuff that was on the parking meters and sitting back down. Totally weird. Is that, like, really research?"

Jefferson made consoling mutterings. Yes, some research was outrageous. And clearly useless. No, he had no idea why it was funded either.

"Of course, I told them that I saw you," said Mary Beth.

Jefferson looked up. "Sorry?"

"Going out for your run, silly. Just before I left for lunch. And I did mention that you were getting much faster, because normally it takes you like two hours to run the two loops around campus you do, but yesterday, you got back by, like, one-ten. So I said to the nice policemen, 'That doesn't surprise me. Professor Daniels is wonderful at everything he does. I bet he is going to become an Olympic marathon runner as well.'"

Jefferson looked confused and then caught sight of the watch on Mary Beth's wrist.

Analog.

He flashed his best smile and asked, "Mary Beth, sweetie, does the big hand point here at 1:10?" as he pointed to the ten on her watch face.

Mary Beth scrunched up her face. "Umm. I think that's right. Yeah. Did I do something wrong? Numbers are so darn confusing."

Jefferson patted her on the hand again. "No, not at all. But I'll let the police know that I'm not trying out for the Olympic squad any time soon."

*****

By one that afternoon, Walter was back at his desk, looking across at Charles Covington III. After all of this was over, Walter would appeal to the Dean for a pay increase. An extra fifty thousand dollars a year was insufficient to deal with all the hassles of being Chair. Walter knew that Charles had not turned up his hearing aids, and he was not going to spend the next forty minutes yelling at the man.

Silently, Walter got out a piece of paper and wrote in large letters "TURN ON YOUR HEARING AIDS. WE NEED TO TALK." He slid the paper across the desk and waited.

Charles read the message, scowled, and finally relented.

"Good," said Walter. "Conversations are so much easier when both sides can hear."

"I'm not retiring," Charles retorted truculently.

"Fine. You teach economic history. It's a meaningless subject that no one cares about. If you want to teach it, that saves me the hassle of hiring someone new. That's not why I asked you here today."

Charles's scowl deepened.

"Charles. I need to know about the ladder," Walter said simply.

"What about it? It's my ladder. It's not hurting you."

"Did you bring it to work yesterday?"

"Sure did. If you did your job properly, I wouldn't've had to."

"What did you do with it?"

"What business is it of yours?"

"It was leaning against the window of a murdered man's office. The man was murdered in *my* department. Now, unfortunately, because of that small detail, *your* ladder is *my* problem."

Charles harrumphed into his mustache. "Well, since you put it like that, I was cleaning out the leaves in the gutters. They were terribly over-full. Could'a damaged the gutters or the drains or worse still, the roof."

Walter stared at Charles. Leaves? There was a ladder up against the window of a murdered man's office because of leaves? There was no point in arguing that leaves in the gutters were the job for the maintenance men. "When were you on the roof?"

"Dunno. Before lunch, because I had lunch at home with Mildred yesterday. So I'd be guessing somewhere between eleven and midday."

Walter nodded. If Charles were telling the truth, the ladder was leaning up against Edmund's window, unattended, between one and two. Anyone could have used it to get in and out of Edmund's office. "Why didn't you take the ladder home with you?"

"Well, don't be telling Mildred, but I got a touch of the vertigo while I was up on the roof, so I couldn't finish the job. So, I just left the ladder there, went home for lunch and rested there for the afternoon as I didn't have any teaching yesterday and figured I'd just finish up the job today."

Walter closed his eyes. The feelings of Charles's wife, Mildred, were the least of his concerns. Images of the elderly professor plunging to his death from the roof because of a vertigo attack flashed before him. That was just what he needed. The Dean, the Provost and the President would definitely want to meet again, if that were to happen.

"Charles," Walter spoke slowly and loudly. "Do not go on the roof again. You could fall off. Let me be clear why this is so important. The injuries you would sustain are inconsequential to me and almost everyone on the planet. The damage to my career, however, would be catastrophic. That is why you need to stay on *terra firma.*

"But," Walter continued, transitioning smoothly into an effortless lie, "to make you feel better, I will make sure someone looks at those leaves. Today."

Charles nodded and got up from the chair slowly. As he left the room he wondered why the Lord made such nasty people. He guessed the same reason the Lord made mosquitoes. As a little reminder that we no longer live in Eden. But it sure was comforting to know that his Creator had a plan for each and every one of the Walters on this earth, and the end for them wasn't going to be pretty.

*****

Tuesday afternoon had begun to fade into an early dusk when the economics faculty, or to be precise, the available faculty, began to drift slowly in for what Walter Scovill had claimed in his email to be an "urgent and important faculty meeting." While the economics faculty at Eaton University numbered over forty at full count, once you subtracted the emeritus, those with research grants, and those on sabbatical, only twenty or so were expected to be in Elm Grove for any given semester.

Gathering Eaton's great thinkers for any meeting was like herding megalomaniacal cats. Each professor proclaimed it was vital that the meeting start on time, but would then arrive whenever convenient to his or her individual schedule, often thirty to forty minutes after the proceedings were slated to begin. Important research or squash games, could not be delayed because of trivial details like student complaints, the university's latest effort to rebrand itself as an elitist college accessible to the masses, provided, of course, that the masses had a spare $80,000 a year, or, as it turned out, the death of a colleague.

Today, Stephen strode into the conference room first, only minutes after the scheduled start time of five p.m. His panic of earlier was gone. In its place was a confident man. Why should he skulk at the back with the junior professors? He, Stephen Choi, should have been awarded tenure. He damn well was going to sit up with the tenured professors where he belonged. What was the worst thing they could do? Fire him? Stephen snorted at the irony of it.

Walter walked in next. He was surprised to see the milkweed was sitting in the tenured faculty seating. A little Rosa Parks revolution in his final days? Well, he, Walter, was on a first name basis with the President of Eaton University. He wasn't going to demean himself by fighting about the location of Stephen Choi's butt.

Walter noted with irritation that the entire faculty, excluding Stephen, was late. The fact he himself had just arrived almost twenty minutes after the hour did not lessen his irritation. It was understood that Walter's time was invaluable. If he was not here, it was because he was somewhere else, attending to Very Important Business. Unlike his lesser colleagues, who just hadn't learned the basic concepts of professional courtesy and punctuality.

With the suffering air of a middle school teacher on a hot Friday afternoon, Walter approached the front of the room and began to look over his notes. He would give them ten more minutes, and then he would begin the meeting, regardless of who was in attendance.

After just a few more minutes, the room began to fill up. It appeared, unlike yesterday, at least three-quarters of the twenty or so available faculty would be in attendance today. Apparently Edmund was a bigger draw card dead than alive.

The seats were laid out in a giant horseshoe, and the junior faculty was sitting at the back, appropriately subordinate (except, of course, for Stephen). The tenured were towards the front, laptops out. This gave the impression they didn't have a minute to waste, an image somewhat tarnished by their frequent coffee breaks in the faculty lounge.

In truth, faculty meetings were typically so boring that the hour was frequently spent catching up on correspondence, poking old friends on Facebook, or writing salacious emails with promises of what was to come later that evening to graduate students, research assistants, or, for the very lucky, nubile, young undergraduates. There had been a memorable six months when the younger gentlemen on the faculty had been addicted to World of Warcraft, raging wars while hunkered down in their offices throughout the day. This may have gone on indefinitely, or at least until the publication review panel met, except a faculty meeting had convened at an inopportune time. Undeterred, the bright young professors just brought their laptops with them. Cries of "oh, you dog" and "nooooo" gave the game away.

Jefferson came in, out of breath and dressed in very short running shorts and a why-bother singlet top, dripping with sweat and drinking another one of his vile looking smoothies. He took a seat on the right-hand side of the horseshoe, at the front, next to Stephen.

Really, that man is insufferable, thought Walter. *How long does it take to towel off and put on a pair of pants? We get it. He has the body of Adonis. Not that big a deal. We all could look like that if we wanted to waste time at the gym.*

Next stomped in Charles, hearing aid volume set at zero.

Nothing in this room worth the price of those darn expensive hearing aid batteries. Just a bunch of pussies wanting to hear themselves talk, thought Charles irritably, as he settled into a seat on the left side of the horseshoe.

Charles was grumpy about not being home to watch *Wheel of Fortune* with Mildred and he wasn't bothering to hide the fact. Ah well, at least he wasn't going to miss his fivesies. Mildred, what a wonderful wife, had dropped off his gin and tonic in a little thermos. Might as well make the best of it and enjoy his cocktail hour and the legs of that nice C.J., if she came.

C.J. made the scene just before Walter's deadline expired. Walter rolled his eyes at the sight of those dreadful cowboy boots. Surely it was only a matter of time before she got married to some cowboy hick and left to bake muffins. Please. Though, Walter admitted, it was tough to imagine the type of man who would be willing to take on a woman like that.

C.J. grabbed an empty Styrofoam coffee cup from the back of the room, went straight to Charles, and yelled in his left ear so he could hear, "Mama's well is dry. Fill 'er up, Pops."

Too shocked to object, Charles poured half his G & T into C.J.'s coffee cup and was rewarded with a kiss on the cheek and a stolen glimpse down her blouse.

"Thanks, darling. The drink was worth the price," she said.

C.J. settled into a seat on the right side of the horseshoe, towards the middle, took a satisfied swallow from the Styrofoam cup, and placed her long legs up on the desk in front of her, causing several of her colleagues to re-adjust uncomfortably in their seats. "Thanks for leaving that info about the position at UT Austin in my mailbox, Walt. But, you know, I love you more than a hog loves mud. So I guess I'll just have to stay here."

Professor Walter Scovill closed his eyes and took several deep breaths. He wasn't picky. These were modern times. She didn't have to marry anyone. He'd settle for the respite of maternity leave. Walter opened his eyes and gave his most ingratiating smile to the faculty. "Thank you for coming. I realize that your time is valuable," he lied. Given the departmental publication rate for the last two years, Walter thought the time of about one-quarter of the people in front of him was valuable-ish, and the rest were disposable goods, but this wasn't the time to get into that.

Walter knew the only thing these people were interested in was Edmund's murder. Heck, that's the only reason why half of them were here. He knew they had off-loaded their first week of teaching onto their graduate students. "Just hand out the syllabus and show the kids the website." Which didn't actually worry Walter that much. Most of the students didn't start class on the first day either, finding their flights "unavoidably delayed" in Belize or St Lucia or Tahiti. But, intrigued by the death of Edmund, it appeared his faculty had hurried, even rushed, back from their exotic vacations or "conferences," a.k.a. university paid speed dating sessions. But Walter wasn't going to pander to such weakness. He didn't want to start by talking about Edmund. He was sick of talking about Edmund. Walter had an agenda, and he was going to stick to it. "The first item on today's agenda is the hiring committee. They are going to give a report on their preliminary progress."

The room fell completely and uncomfortably silent. There wasn't even the clicking of a keyboard. No one looked at Stephen. Everyone knew they were talking about hiring his replacement. Then the murmurings began.

C.J. just cut her eyes at Walter. Jerk. This matter could, and should, be handled at a meeting of the tenured faculty, out of Stephen's hearing.

Walter tried to regain control. Condescension to his colleagues was his favored method, though he was never above yelling. "Jefferson, I couldn't hear you. Did you say something you wished to share?"

"I was just saying that I was glad that I wasn't on the hiring committee, as their workload has doubled. I assume we are going to hire a replacement for Edmund's position."

Chatter broke out among the room again.

"Do you think the killer will strike again?"

"Are we all at risk?"

"Do you think we could get that guy from Harvard, if we got him a bodyguard as well?"

"I think there is an up and coming grad student at Stanford we should look at."

C.J. said a silent thank-you to Jefferson for drawing the attention away from Stephen.

Peter Johansson stood up and finally quieted the room with a series of restrained coughs. Peter Johansson was a graying man in his early fifties, with a disconcerting habit of rubbing his balding head as if searching for his lost follicles. His befuddled demeanor often gave the impression of a kindly soul. However, like most economists, Peter Johansson viewed kindness as an input, a means of achieving his own agenda.

"Umm. So, for those of you who don't know, I am Chair of the Hiring Committee. Despite having met several times over the summer, we have only just begun the process of the search for the new junior faculty member. It seems industrial organization professors just study organization. I don't seem to have the quality of organization myself."

Peter chuckled at his little joke. No one else did. Peter massaged his scalp but finding no hair continued self-consciously. "Umm. Yes. Well, as I was saying, there isn't much to report. As for a second position, clearly, we have to see what the budget is for Edmund's position and, umm, the risk averseness of the candidate."

Again, Peter gave a little chuckle.

Snickers of laughter reluctantly broke out around the room. It wasn't clear if they were laughing at the appalling microeconomics joke or the idea that the next hire would also die. Though, it soon became apparent where the focus of the room was.

People threw out suggestions of colleagues whom they didn't like who should be offered the position. One person asked if the department could offer the position to his wife, as his divorce was costing him a packet. Others, irritated by the graduate students they had to supervise, offered them up as bait. Jefferson observed dryly that his sympathy for the hiring committee was perhaps misplaced. It seemed there were plenty of candidates.

Walter banged his fist on the desk, trying to call the meeting back to order. "Let's hope the hiring committee has more progress to report next time," Walter said acidly. "I am sure they don't want to have to increase their teaching loads to cover the shortfall. The second agenda item is who is going to teach the Econ 101 class, which is now unexpectedly without a professor. The class takes place on Mondays and Wednesdays at nine a.m. Any volunteers?"

Now the room was deathly quiet. No one berated Walter for not mentioning that the class was without a professor because that professor had been murdered. To do so might draw unwanted attention and, therefore, the responsibility of teaching the class. Instead, people looked intently at their computer screens, studied their cuticles, seemed fascinated to discover they had shoelaces, and were amazed by the number of wrinkles on the backs of their hands.

After a minute or so of very uncomfortable silence, Walter smiled. "Well, C.J.," Walter said in an overly cheery tone, "since you love me as much a...what was the phrase exactly...'hog loves mud' I think...I am quite sure you won't mind doing me this little favor. Would you?"

C.J. had not climbed this high in a male dominated profession for no reason. She did not display her emotions, regardless of how she felt. And right now she was furious. Edmund's class was on Mondays and Wednesdays. Her class was on Tuesdays and Thursdays. Now she would be teaching all four days, with little time for research. "Oh Walt. You just go and sign me right up, sugar."

Walter smiled victoriously. He would needle that Tex Mex disaster into resigning one of these days. If it was the last thing he did.

Walter then peered down at his notes, unsure how to introduce the third agenda item. Now he couldn't avoid the topic of Edmund dying so inconveniently in the department. "As you know, our dear friend and colleague Edmund DeBeyer has...passed on."

People looked up from their computer screens. It was a bit late in the meeting to start expressing sympathy now. What was Walter up to?

"His funeral will be tomorrow night at the Triunity Church on the Square. Seven o'clock start."

C.J. wondered how the body had been released from autopsy so quickly. Maybe the forensic lab had liked spending time with Edmund as much as his work colleagues had. Or, perhaps more likely, The Ego had jumped the queue, thanks to the Eaton University powers that be.

Walter looked down at his notes again and shuffled his papers awkwardly. "Also, the Provost and the college," Walter stopped. That didn't sound right. That sounded like he was doing the bidding of others.

Walter continued, speaking slowly and deliberately, "I am concerned about how the...passing...of Edmund is affecting your..." Walter paused, searching for the right word, "mental equilibrium."

C.J. snorted with laughter. A few other chuckles and snickers were also heard.

Walter glared the room back into silence. "I am here to discuss the options available to you to ensure your... wellbeing. Um. I am going to make available someone for you to talk to...and a...a...dog."

The room stared back at Walter.

Finally C.J. broke the silence. "Walt," she said casually, "I don't need a shrink or a puppy, for that matter, to help me deal with the fact that I don't have to work with our beloved Edmund anymore. I shed that tear at the celebration party I threw. What I do need help with is how you expect me to be a happy, productive, clucky chicken in this darling little hen house when I know that the fox is still lurking amongst us."

Murmurs of assent broke out among the room. A few people banged on the desks to show their support. A "Here, here!" came from a junior faculty at the back, who promptly slid down in his seat from the shame of being so bold.

Charles, sensing something exciting was finally happening by the attitudes of those around him, the fist banging and the look on Walter's face, turned on his hearing aids. If there was gossip on the agenda, he didn't want to miss it. Mildred loved a good, department gossip story. He asked his neighbor loudly, so loudly the entire room could hear, "Hey, what's this? What's the fuss?"

Before his neighbor could answer, C.J. called out from across the room. "I'm causing the fuss, Charles. I want to know if one of us is the murderer. It would make it so much more enjoyable to come to faculty meetings, don't you think, if you weren't worried about being strangled?"

A few faculty laughed. Others started to glance around the room, sizing up their fellow workers as potential stranglers. More than one was condemned.

Charles, his tongue loosened by his fivesie, replied with great enthusiasm, "It's the money, my dear C.J. Follow the money and you'll find your strangler. Happens all the time, people killing for money. There was that Lizzie Borden, though she got away with it. And look at those Menendez brothers out in California. Couldn't wait a week to start spending their parents' money on flashy cars and clothes which made it all rather obvious. Brains the size of peas, if you ask me. Our Lord and Creator, for whatever reason, blessed Edmund with a rather sizeable fortune. You should be asking, 'Who benefitted from the will?'"

Walter smiled. As Edmund's quest for power and control rivaled his own, the two men had worked together as well as two bull elephants in musth. He was going to enjoy this announcement. "Thanks for raising that, Charles," Walter said generously. "The issue of Edmund's will is our final agenda item today. Edmund left his fortune to…himself."

Jefferson looked pale. "Does he want to be frozen and brought back to life?"

"Thank God, no," Water reassured him. "Though I am sure the idea crossed his mind. But I think even Edmund realized that in 50 years, or 100, or whenever they brought him back, he would no longer be the leading researcher in his field, and that would be unbearable. No. But I have spoken to his wife, Lisa, today, and interestingly, his will doesn't leave a penny to her, but instead sets up the Edmund DeBeyer Memorial Foundation. The foundation's mission is to preserve his intellectual legacy, rather than his body."

C.J. interjected. "Well, his wife might not have had a motive to kill him while he was alive. But she sure has a motive to kill him now that he's dead."

Walter continued, ignoring C.J., "The foundation will set up a library, featuring Edmund's works and others who cite Edmund's work. There is also to be a research foundation for promising scholars who will continue to further Edmund's research. The scholars must be graduate students or junior professors, so," Walter turned and looked at Jefferson, "even though your research is so closely aligned with Edmund's, I am afraid you can't benefit from the funds, Jefferson."

Jefferson just nodded his head in acknowledgment.

The new, confident Stephen, who had been rather quiet until now, could no longer contain himself. "Good God! The man has set up his will to inflate his citation count, even after he's dead."

"Well, think how much fun we can have at the Christmas party," soothed C.J., "playing 'Guess how many citations Edmund has now?' But Walter, dear, you are bringing this up because, why? My guess is there is a clause saying it has to be housed here."

"Well...yes. In fact, it states it has to be housed in 40 Knollwood. At the moment, the obvious choice is Edmund and Jefferson's offices as they are next to each other and the only offices on the top floor of 40 Knollwood. It would be an easy renovation."

Jefferson looked up, aghast. "Do we have to accept this...thing?" asked Jefferson, obviously deeply disturbed at the idea of losing his office for a foundation from which he could not gain.

"No, not technically," said Walter. "But it is unlikely we would turn down that much research money for our graduate students and junior faculty."

Just at that moment, the doors to the conference room opened, and two Elm Grove policemen walked in.

Walter didn't look impressed. This was his faculty meeting. Pompously he turned to the officers. "Gentleman, we are discussing matters critical to the economics department of Eaton University. If you would like to question any one of us to gather further information, we will, of course, cooperate. We will be concluding our business in approximately ten minutes, and then we can turn our attention to yours."

The policemen didn't even acknowledge Walter, but instead walked straight up to Stephen. "Stephen Choi. You are under arrest for the murder of Edmund DeBeyer. You have the right to remain silent. Anything you say or do can and will be held against you in a court of law. You have the right to an attorney. If you cannot afford an attorney, one will be provided for you. Do you understand these rights I have just read to you?"

Stephen, his new-found bravado replaced with shock and fright, looked wildly around the room as the cuffs were placed on his wrists. "What? I didn't do this!" he cried. "I didn't murder Edmund. This isn't true!"

WEDNESDAY

Despite professing feelings of porcine delight to Walter only the day before, nothing about C.J.'s demeanor on Wednesday morning resembled a happy pig in mud. Rather, she approached the Economics 101 classroom like an irritated bull at an overcrowded rodeo. Pity the eighteen-year-old fool who thought he could get the better of her that day, even for eight seconds. Lack of sleep did that to a girl. Edmund had prepared nothing for the course. Zilch. Nada. Consequently, C.J., who had not yet developed a complete professorial indifference to her students, had been up until the small hours writing a syllabus, lecture and problem set.

The only saving grace in the whole damn fiasco was the fact that Jose was the teaching assistant for the course. That boy at least had some brains and wasn't afraid of a little work. Which was good, as C.J. wasn't going to get carried away with her teaching obligations and grade an undergraduate essay herself. Would a five-star chef dice an onion?

C.J. did not want to think about how old and haggard she looked, thanks to her late night Econ 101 prep session. C.J. realized that in the eyes of her eighteen-year-old students, she looked fifty on a good day. Today she would be fortunate to escape without being asked if she needed assistance crossing the road.

What a shame Edmund is already dead, C.J. thought bitterly as she tried to blink life into her gritty, tired eyes. *I would so enjoy killing him myself this morning.*

No matter. It was still open season on Walter Scovill.

C.J. strode purposefully to the front of the lecture hall with her pink cowboy boots clicking loudly and hair flying wildly behind her.

"I am Professor Whitmore. As I am sure you all know, Professor DeBeyer is not teaching the rest of the semester for the obvious reason that he is dead. I encourage each and every one of you, as you process your grief, to see the head of the econ department, Professor Walter Scovill. He has *assured* me he would *love* to talk with every one of you, *individually*, about this *at length*. His room number, phone number, website and email are on the syllabus I am passing out to you."

C.J. paused and scanned the room. One face looked vaguely familiar, but C.J. couldn't place where she had seen the girl. Probably in Wallaby's. More notable was that despite the fact their professor had just been murdered, no one appeared upset or grieving, unless the youth of today grieved by flirting with their neighbors. C.J. hoped this small detail wouldn't keep down the number of students stopping by Walter's office. Her revenge enacted, C.J. started the lecture for the day.

Less than a minute later, she stopped and stared stone-faced at the class. The whole time she had been enlightening them on the delights of the demand curve, C.J. was aware she had not had their full attention. Single girls in low cut tank tops batted their eyelash extensions at the tattooed biceps sitting next to them. Other students clustered like mushrooms around small screens indiscreetly hidden under desks, exchanging morning gossip.

"Did she really?"

"I heard he wanted it."

"But what about Aimee??"

The classroom valentines were connected by common ear buds and, disconcertingly, hands and tongues. For most, the learning of economics seemed to be of secondary or, in some cases, tertiary, importance.

C.J. waited the class out for their attention. She waited until the whispering and giggling and fondling died down. She waited until all the ear buds were removed. She waited until the last students looked up from their iPhones. Then, she waited some more. She had not had their attention before, but she sure did now. They shifted uncomfortably in their seats. This strange lady in her pink cowboy boots looked pissed.

"You know," C.J. drawled benignly in her full Texas twang, eventually breaking the painful silence, "I get a pretty good view of y'all from here at the podium. Not great. But pretty good. For instance, I can see when your hands are in your lap and you get that happy, little smile on your face."

C.J. paused and looked around from student to student. Most students were looking puzzled, not sure where she was going with this speech. Some were clearly annoyed. C.J. was wasting their valuable, trust-fund time.

"But the view isn't that great," C.J. continued, in the tone of one telling a quaint Texas folktale. "For example, I can't tell what your sweet little hands are doing. When someone's hands are in their lap and they're smiling all happy like, I got two guesses. They're textin' or they're masturbatin'."

Students gasped. Had the professor really just said the m-word? OMG! Who was this woman?

"Now, I got to say, it don't really matter which one you're doing, because neither are okay in an Eaton University lecture hall. So, let's be real clear. If your hands are below the desk, you will be asked to leave. And if I have to discuss why you were asked to leave class with your fine parents who are paying cold, hard cash for you to sit here and learn, I will tell them it looked like you were pleasuring yourself in my classroom. Now, I am sure I have been clear."

Students nodded dumbly, placing their cell phones and iPads in their backpacks and their hands on their notebooks. Their faces showed their shock at having their technology removed from them and in such a dramatic fashion.

C.J., however, was thinking something else. *These students are technology addicted. Technology. Stephen used a lot of technology. I wonder.... Is there a digital yellow brick road to showing that Stephen is innocent?*

Drawn back to the present by the silent stares, some sullen, some wide-eyed, of the phone-free students, C.J. gave them a great big Texan smile. "Now, that's just wonderful. Getting back to the demand curve. Looking around the room, I get the feeling there has been an increase in demand for tattoos over recent years. Anyone got a particularly good one on an arm or a leg they want to show?"

*****

"I knew it!" exclaimed Betsy loudly, as C.J. entered Wallaby's at just after eleven.

C.J. just shook her head and went over to order a caramel latte, extra cream. It was that kind of day.

Betsy, C.J. noticed, was not knitting today. Instead, she had just put aside a copy of *The Pug Post*. The arrest of a colleague meant Betsy's role as sleuth superseded that of grandmother. As C.J. sat down next to her friend, drink in hand, she glanced over to see the *The Pug's* headline of the day. "CHOI-KED TO DEATH!" Ouch.

Betsy, wobbling like a Jell-O cup with excitement, continued talking. "Stephen was the lemon! All those Chinese death rituals, all that bitterness over not getting tenure. He snuck out of his office and strangled Edmund."

"Would it matter to your conclusion if I told you that Stephen was *not* in his office the hour before Edmund died? But instead he was walking downtown at about one o'clock?"

Betsy looked puzzled. "But, I don't understand. Stephen said he was in his office. Has he changed his story?"

"Not on purpose. But Mary Beth saw him walking into downtown and told Jefferson, and Jeffie told me after the faculty meeting last night. As you know, nothing is secret in an academic department."

C.J. took a long sip of caramel-flavored coffee, savoring two of her favorite food groups, caffeine and sugar. Then she turned to Betsy and asked thoughtfully, "Why would Stephen walk downtown at one o'clock if he wanted to kill Edmund a few minutes later?"

"To give himself an alibi, of course."

"But then, why lie about it?"

Betsy was quiet for a moment, thinking this new development through.

"Exactly," said C.J. "I think the fact Stephen lied about being in his office shows that he is innocent. Obviously he left his office at lunchtime for some reason. But not to give himself an alibi. Whatever he was doing, it wasn't killing Edmund."

Betsy still looked skeptical. "Well," Betsy said finally, "why doesn't he just say where he was? Then he wouldn't be sitting in jail right now."

C.J. sighed deeply, looking troubled. "Betsy, dear, you have struck at the fundamental problem. I, like you, have been assuming that all of the innocent people in this affair would do everything they could to prove that they were innocent. It seemed the rational choice. But why are we assuming that everyone is going to behave rationally? What are we? Nineteenth-century economic theorists, like Walter? I think emotions, like embarrassment or love, are coming in to play."

Betsy looked confused, so C.J. continued her explanation in simpler terms. "My guess is Stephen doesn't want anyone to know what he was up to on Monday afternoon because he was doing something... naughty...or...or perhaps his afternoon activities reveal something about someone else."

"Oh. I get you," said Betsy, with the air of sudden understanding. "It is possible he might have been seeing a...well, you know, an escort...at one of the hotels downtown. How strange he won't say anything. It's not like an economist to have that much honor or delicacy, for that matter. But you never can tell with, you know...Asians. Their culture is very different."

She sighed, clearly disappointed to have to give up on her first suspect. "It's often not the first one they arrest on *Law and Order,* either. But if it isn't Stephen, who is it?"

C.J. decided to ignore Betsy's comment about Stephen's cultural background as she thought inwardly, *You just can never tell with old people.* Instead, she batted her eyes innocently. "My dear Betsy. What are you saying? That more than one person might have wanted to kill dearest Edmund?"

Betsy chuckled. "Well, I don't like to speak ill of the dead..."

"I know. I know. It's easier to ask who didn't have a motive. I was talking with Jefferson earlier, and he said he had heard that the police had confirmed that Lisa DeBeyer was at the gallery in New York, so the wife didn't do it. Which leaves Stephen, Charles, Jefferson, Walter and myself as the only faculty not on vacation, at home, or teaching. Stephen had a motive. Edmund had denied his tenure. That's why the poor chap is dressed in an orange jump suit as we speak. But assuming it's not Stephen...Charles had a motive. Edmund was angling to get him kicked off the faculty."

"But Charles was at home."

"Walter had plenty of motive. Edmund had clearly passed Walter in the department's ego to brain ratio race. I am sure Walter has been wanting the man dead for years."

Again Betsy demurred. "But Walter was in his office. And why kill him now, after all this time?"

C.J. pursed her lips. "I sure would like Walter's alibi corroborated, anyhow."

"Well, I don't think it was Walter. If it wasn't Stephen, I think Jefferson killed Edmund," Betsy declared confidently.

"Jefferson?" asked C.J. wonderingly.

"Yes," said Betsy firmly. "On *Law and Order*, it is always the person you least suspect. And I don't suspect Jefferson at all. Frankly, he is the only person in the department who is showing any grief. He looks like he hasn't had any sleep since it happened."

"Jefferson?" asked C.J. again. "How would he have done it? He was out running at the time Edmund was killed."

"That's not a problem. He was running laps of the campus, so he could have run one lap, dashed back to Edmund's office, killed Edmund, and then dashed out again and continued on with the second lap of his run."

"But why? Jefferson is the one person who has a productive working relationship with Edmund. It seems unlikely that he decides to suddenly kill his coauthor in the middle of a run. Very unlikely."

"Mmmm," mused Betsy. "I see what you mean. But I still think it's Jefferson."

*****

Two coffees and a scone later, and feeling quite rejuvenated, C.J. went to leave Wallaby's at close on midday. As she was heading out the door, C.J. almost bumped into Annika Jonsdottir. The girl had paid for her coffee and was clearly distracted, walking hastily and talking to herself. By the expression on her face, C.J. could tell the girl was troubled.

"Annika?" C.J. asked questioningly. Inwardly, C.J. sighed. She hated dealing with student troubles.

"Oh!" cried Annika with a start. "Professor Whitmore. You startle me."

"I see that. Is everything alright? You look... concerned...about something."

"Me? Oh, no. Me? I am fine. I am just, um... thinking about...Professor Daniels's problem set. Excuse me, Professor Whitmore. I must go."

With that, the young woman scurried off down the street, leaving C.J. staring after her, unsure of what she had just seen.

A large gust of wind startled C.J. from her reverie. The clouds in the sky were building and had turned a menacing shade of slate grey. C.J. had no idea why the founding fathers decided to settle around New England. Surely it wasn't for the weather. Long, dragging winters that were suddenly replaced in May by hot, humid summers (apparently missing spring altogether). Summers that eventually eased into fall with its torrential rains from the hurricane season. And it looked as if one of those rains was moving in tonight.

Really, thought C.J., forgetting all about Annika and focusing entirely on the storm overhead, *would it have killed the founding fathers to settle in Hawaii first? Then, maybe Eaton University would have been founded there.*

*****

Mary Beth loved lunchtime. She was always ready to leave the confines of the office. She loved to visit the different lunch spots around campus and read *Cosmo* and *People* and *Us Weekly*. Mary Beth reveled in celebrity gossip, especially the break ups, and took careful note of the hairstyle tips and beauty advice. She knew you couldn't let yourself go, and, with that in mind, Mary Beth decided that the current Mourning Manicure had run its course. She would need a Funeral Manicure before tonight, even if it meant using an Elm Grove manicurist.

Today, Mary Beth was heading to Zoe's. The deli was one of her favorite places in town. Delicious food, but not too fattening. No rich husband was going to want a chubby wife.

Leaving the office, Mary Beth was stopped by a strong wind. She did a quick outfit check. Did she have a coat in the office cute enough to wear to lunch? Deciding she didn't, and it was better to freeze and look cute rather than be warm and ugly, Mary Beth continued down the street.

Mary Beth spotted Professor Whitmore walking towards her. Now, that woman was unmarried for a reason. Didn't she own a mirror? What was she thinking with those pink cowboy boots and loud spangled cowgirl shirts and skirts? Underneath the fashion accident that was her wardrobe, there was a relatively attractive woman. Mary Beth had considered sending in C.J.'s name to *Extreme Makeover*. But people can be so sensitive, even when you are doing them a huge favor.

"Hey, Mary Beth," called C.J. loudly. It seemed to Mary Beth that C.J. did everything loudly—another reason she would not get a husband. *Cosmo* was very clear. Demure and soothing would win the day. Well, it was probably just as well that C.J. was loud and ugly. Less competition for Mary Beth.

Mary Beth responded to C.J. with a large, toothy smile, somewhat like a cat spotting a tasty mouse. She had wanted to talk with C.J. and get her take on the events of the last few days. This was the perfect opportunity, out of the office and the big ears that lurked around every turn. "Hey, Professor Whitmore," said Mary Beth, in her most welcoming tone. "What a fabulous shirt. I love that color….magenta is it? Are you grabbing some lunch?"

"Oh no. I just had coffee with a friend. I'm heading back to work."

"Darn. I'm running out to Zoe's. Have you checked it out?"

C.J. confessed that she didn't know Zoe's, but the two women agreed that they would have lunch together there someday, while each of them knew this would never happen.

"Hey, I'm like, um, still too scared to sleep because of Professor DeBeyer. Is it true? Was Professor Choi arrested?" Mary Beth asked, fishing for information. "Because, you know, I saw him walking into town when I was at lunch on Monday. It's like, too freaky that we've been risking our lives working with a serial killer."

C.J., as she liked to say herself, was not new to the barn. She inwardly rolled her eyes at Mary Beth's supposed fright. The young woman standing before C.J. looked very well-rested. "I can say with certainty that your life has not been in danger from a serial killer, at least not yet," C.J. said dryly, though at the same time wondering why not and thinking it wouldn't bother her if the real killer wanted to elevate himself to the status of serial killing if it meant he would kill Mary Beth. Wasn't there someone in the world who was sufficiently annoyed with this walking manicure to do her in?

"Well, you never know. I knew Professor Choi was a murderer, even before he killed Professor DeBeyer."

C.J. just raised her eyebrows.

"You know, he like, had that murderous look."

C.J. wondered if the murderous look Mary Beth was referring to was the fact that Stephen was Asian and, therefore, looked different to Mary Beth. As Stephen was a practicing Buddhist, C.J. could not imagine Mary Beth had seen Stephen wandering around the department with looks of murderous rage on his face frequently. Though, in Mary Beth's defense, Stephen was prone to be moody. "No. I'm not quite sure I know," murmured C.J.

"Oh, yes. And then he had that terrible temper. Why, just on the day of the murder, he got into a terrible fight with Professor DeBeyer."

Now Mary Beth had C.J.'s attention. "A fight? When?"

"After lunch. I had come back from my lunch and was going up to Professor DeBeyer's office to drop off the letters I had typed for him..."

C.J. interrupted. "What time was this?"

"That's the thing. Time is, like, so confusing. I'm supposed to be back from lunch at exactly one. But I was running a few minutes late, as I had to finish reading this article in *Us Weekly* about new ways to style your hair that will drive your man wild. Though I'm not sure a hair style is what guys are into, you know? I find that a push-up bra and a scoop tee work pretty good."

C.J. cleared her throat. "You got back to the office?"

Mary Beth looked at C.J. blankly for a moment. "Oh right. Yeah. So, I got back to the office, a little late. And then, I had to find the letters. I was sure I had left them on the tray on the right side of my desk. But there they were, on the left side, after all. So my best guess is that it was about when the big hand was pointing to the two or the three."

C.J. just stared.

"I have this new watch, you see," explained Mary Beth, seeing C.J.'s confusion. "It has a face. But it's like super confusing as it doesn't actually say the time."

Mary Beth showed C.J. her analog watch, and C.J. could see at once that Mary Beth was saying that she went to Edmund's office between ten past and fifteen past one. "Ahh. I see. So you went up with the letters …and then what happened?"

"Well, I could hear Edmund yelling something awful. But only when I got right up close to the door, mind. Those offices are built like fortresses. I wish my apartment was that sound proof. The things I hear my neighbors doing. TMI, that's all I can say."

C.J., not at all interested in the sex lives of Mary Beth's neighbors, tried to steer the conversation back. "But at Edmund's door..."

"Oooh, yes. I heard Professor DeBeyer in a right old dust up with Professor Choi. He must have said something to make Professor DeBeyer real mad because Professor DeBeyer yelled 'You're finished, you hear me, you are finished!'"

C.J. waited, expecting more, but Mary Beth was clearly done.

"What happened after you heard Professor DeBeyer yell that?" asked C.J.

"Well, it obviously wasn't the time to drop off the letters, so I went back down to my office."

C.J. stared at the girl for a few moments. "Mary Beth. Let me make sure I understand. On the day Professor DeBeyer was murdered, you told Professor Daniels that you saw Stephen Choi walking downtown while you were sitting at Bruegger's Bagels at a few minutes before one o'clock. And now you are telling me that sometime between 1:10 and 1:15 p.m. on the same day, you overheard Professor DeBeyer yelling a threatening statement at someone. But you didn't see that someone or hear that someone. So, you don't know who that someone was or even if that someone was in the room with him. That person could have been on the phone."

Mary Beth couldn't contain herself any longer. "But, we do know it was Professor Choi who was in the office arguing, Professor Whitmore," said Mary Beth, with the tone of one explaining basic math to a child. Again. "It was Professor Choi because he's the killer. It's not my job to explain how he did it. I guess he ran back really quickly. Professor Choi had such a bad temper he provoked Professor DeBeyer into an argument and then killed him. And that doesn't surprise me. I always knew he had the look of a killer."

C.J. looked at Mary Beth with a long, thoughtful stare. "Mary Beth," she eventually asked, "did you see Stephen Choi come back to the department at any time on the afternoon Professor DeBeyer was murdered?"

"Oh yes!" said Mary Beth with a cheerful lack of concern. "About two-ish, I'd say. He came rushing in to 40 Knollwood to go to the seminar. But I couldn't say if he'd come from his office or downtown. Not that it matters. He'd, like, already done the deed by then."

*****

Later that afternoon, sitting in her office, C.J. opened her Google page. Stephen, being under the age of fifty, was also a complete Google addict. Gmail, Google Play, Google Docs, and, of course, Google Calendar.

She set about hacking his Google account. She entered his email address and then experimented with passwords.

Choi1

Too short. What was the minimum length? C.J. guessed six or eight characters.

Choi12

Nope again.

Choi1234

Bingo!

Ah. It was great to have colleagues with no lives outside the office. No chance for passwords named after much-loved pets, Star Trek characters or motorcycles ridden in a misspent youth. Of course, it takes one to know one. C.J.'s own password, from Amazon to Netflix to Wells Fargo, was CJWhit12. A hackers dream.

Successful with Choi1234, C.J. was in, looking at all of Stephen's documents, email, and calendar. She was sure that access should have been frozen by the police but she was guessing that they were still thinking of computers as items with a hard drive. Not shells used to access the cloud.

She went straight to the calendar. Monday, 1 p.m.— 2 p.m: G.A. Not much help. C.J. couldn't think of anyone on the faculty with those initials. C.J. racked her brains. *G.A.: G*rade *A*cademic papers. (Unlikely on the first day of semester.); *G*olf with *A*dam. (Did Stephen even play golf? C.J. didn't think so.); *G*ive *A*lms. (Unlikely. Any economist knows you donate to the poor on December 31st.) But at least it didn't say "Murder Edmund" she thought ironically.

C.J. started to look through Stephen's emails, his documents, his playlist and his recent book purchases. She had never realized he liked funk-fusion jazz. Or, embarrassingly, that the man was Korean, not Chinese. As C.J. read Stephen's email, she was amazed to discover he had a girlfriend who was a graduate student at the University of California at Berkeley. What else didn't she know about him?

C.J. spent some time clicking her way through his documents, not finding much of anything. Some uninspiring research papers, a few rather boring Powerpoint slides for teaching and a rather mysterious, half-written letter of apology addressed to herself. But then, C.J. clicked on an innocuous-looking document buried deep in a research folder, labeled "Statistics."

Sadly, as a statistician herself, C.J. understood what she was looking at. She clicked around Stephen's folders, looking for more evidence. Now the apology letter made sense. And she was certain she knew who G.A. was and why Stephen wasn't saying anything.

*****

Many people thought the Triunity Church, located on the north edge of the large sloping lawn of the Elm Grove Town Square, was spectacular. To be sure, the church was a striking example of the gothic architecture that littered the streets of Elm Grove. The outside of the church was somber, heavy-set grey stone, but the inside was where it shone. Cathedral ceilings gleamed with polished wood and graceful arches. Stained glass windows cast rainbows of lights throughout. Rows of traditional wooden pews lined a protracted center aisle, making the church an ideal choice for the Elm Grove bride looking for a lengthy walk to Pachelbel's Canon.

By seven o'clock on Wednesday night, the storm had moved over Elm Grove in earnest. Unrelenting, heavy rain fell, and strong winds rattled windows and doors. Edmund's casket, covered with pale blue forget-me-nots (*"As if we ever could,"* whispered C.J. to Betsy *when she saw the choice of flower.*), was set at the front of the Triunity Church. As C.J. and Betsy entered the church, they could see the church was filling with Eaton University dignitaries *("Oh look,"* said Betsy, *"that's the President of Eaton University himself over there."*), the faculty and staff of the economics department, plus many others from colleges and universities around the country. *("How many economists does it take to change a light bulb?" C.J. joked to Betsy. Betsy shook her head in disbelief and made shushing noises. "Two. One to assume the existence of the ladder, and one to change the light bulb."*) Some of the hungrier graduate students were also in attendance, looking for free food. And of course, the police were quietly hovering in the background. *("See? They don't think it's Stephen, either," whispered Betsy with delight. "They're here to spot the killer."*)

C.J. wondered how Edmund would have felt about a Wednesday night funeral. To realize that, in death, he was an inconvenience to be slotted in between two busy days in the opening week of the semester, days filled with teaching, faculty meetings and committee obligations that no one wanted to reschedule. Perhaps more to the point, the Eaton Media Machine had decided that it was best to bury him and the story of his murder as quickly as possible. *But,* she thought somewhat wistfully, looking around the church filled with the who's who of Eaton University, *even on this miserable night, Edmund can still pull a crowd. He would have liked that.*

Right by the casket, alone, was a tall, striking woman, about thirty years old, who appeared to be completely at ease in her five inch Prada shoes and well-cut designer black dress. Her hair, a light strawberry-blonde, hung in waves of light curls down her back, and delicate curls framed her face. Most strikingly, her tearless, pale blue eyes scanned the crowd with intensity.

*****

"Who is that woman?" Trudy Scovill asked her husband, Walter, while shifting her rather hefty weight from foot to foot. Her feet were killing her. She hadn't worn heels this high since her wedding day, and that was a good twenty-five years ago.

"Which woman?" asked Walter, without even looking at his wife. Not a patient man normally, Walter had no tolerance for his wife's trifling queries tonight. He had tried every argument to persuade Trudy not to attend the festivities, appealing to Trudy's need to be entertained ("*You'll be bored by the sermon.*"), to her social snobbery ("*The man didn't have any family of significance.*") and to the usual stalwart, fashion ("*You'll ruin your new shoes in the rain.*"). But Mrs. Trudy Scovill was not to be deterred. It's not every day you get to go to the funeral of a murdered man. She was not going to be cheated out of such an event. Besides, she wanted to talk to the other faculty wives. She wanted to know what their husbands thought about Stephen being the killer and about Edmund's will. All that money and he didn't leave a penny of it to his wife. She had checked on Walter's will as soon as she had heard.

Walter did not care about some lady his wife had spotted. Walter had already been stopped by the President of the college and the Provost, each wanting to reinforce that it was Walter's responsibility to make sure this mess did not affect the Great State of Eaton. Walter knew it was only a matter of minutes before he ran into the Dean. "*Yes, Sir. Of course, Sir. What a great idea, Sir,*" Walter practiced saying bitterly in his mind.

"That one. The pretty one by the body," persisted Trudy, pointing rather obviously to the woman with the strawberry-blonde hair.

Walter, relenting, looked in the direction Trudy was indicating. "Oh, her. That's Edmund's wife, of course. Linda. No. Lisle. No...um...wait...Lisa. Yes. That's it. Lisa. You don't see her much about the department. She does something with art, in New York City. I think she lives there most of the time."

"Really?" cooed Trudy with interest. "She's much younger than he is. Was. Edmund, I mean. You would never have thought he would have been the type."

"And what type is that, dear?"

"You know. The type of older man who likes younger women...and can get them. I mean, all older men like younger women, but not all of them have the charisma to land them. Edmund didn't strike me as having that much...charm."

"Well, I suppose he could be nice if he wanted to."

"Hmmm. How long where they married?"

Walter looked at his wife blankly. "I don't know. Five years? Maybe ten? Who knows? What does it matter?"

"Well, I suppose it's not that important. Do they have any kids?"

Walter snorted in exasperation. "What is this? Twenty Questions? How the hell am I supposed to know? I doubt it. I've never heard of any."

Walter's wife was unperturbed by his rudeness. After so many years together she was used to it. "Well, maybe it's for the best that there aren't any little ones. But for right now, she is clearly standing there by the casket, waiting to be received, and no one is going over. She keeps looking around, to see if anyone will come by. I think, as Chair of the department you should start things off."

"What are you talking about?"

"Really, Walter. For someone who is supposed to be smart, I wonder about you sometimes. At a funeral, the widow stands by the deceased, and the people at the funeral go and say something to comfort her. Why every single academic in this room doesn't know this, I can't, for the life of me, figure out."

"Well, I'm not sure how many know that Lisa is his wife," excused Walter lamely.

Trudy pushed Walter in the direction of the lonely widow and then took it upon herself to round up a few more people to join the receiving line. After all, she was the wife of the Chair of the department. First Lady of the department as it were. This role did carry with it certain responsibilities.

She quickly spotted C.J. and Betsy and sent them along. *Who could miss C.J.?* she thought, looking at C.J.'s outfit. *Pink cowboy boots? At a funeral? Really?* Then old Charles Covington and his wife joined the line, delighted at the prospect of meeting the young Mrs. DeBeyer.

Trudy also stumbled upon that terrible secretary, dressed like a slut as always. What was her name? Mary Something. Mary Ann? No. Mary Kate? Well, whatever. She looked liked she had forgotten half of her clothes at home today. It was disgraceful.

Trudy did not think Mary Beth was appropriate receiving line material, but Mary Beth, seeing a line beginning to form, was not to be discouraged.

"It's Mrs. Walter, isn't it?" she asked Trudy.

"Yes, dearie," Trudy said, without a lot of enthusiasm.

"It looks like we can go and view the body now. How exciting. It was getting a little boring, just standing around. I'm going to hop right in line, so I don't miss my chance."

And before Trudy could say anything, Mary Beth toddled towards the front of the church in knee-high, black boots with well-toned butt cheeks peeking from the bottom of her black mini skirt in the most tantalizing manner.

As Trudy waddled toward the mourners, looking for sufficiently distinguished grievers for Mrs. DeBeyer, she noticed that nice Jose and a young woman she assumed was his girlfriend joining the line. Trudy liked Jose. He was always such a helpful young man and a very hard worker. Well, they weren't exactly the caliber of people she had in mind for Mrs. DeBeyer, but Jose was always very clean and respectful. She would let him and his girlfriend stay in the receiving line.

*****

Closer to the casket, Walter was deep in conversation with Lisa. Speaking in low, consoling tones, no one else could hear what he was saying. But C.J. couldn't help wondering what he was rambling on about, as Lisa had the searching look of woman about to fling herself through the first fire exit she found, alarm bells be damned.

In the receiving line, Betsy was telling Charles about how Freddie, one of the middle grandchildren, was starring as Willie Wonka in the fifth grade play. Charles, fresh drink in hand, was nodding amicably, though not hearing a word. But that was really all the encouragement Betsy needed, and she was launching into details about costumes, the number of lines, and how Freddie was chosen instead of Oliver, another young boy whom everyone thought was a certainty for the lead, given that he took acting lessons, and his mother was the head of the PTA.

C.J. herself was talking with Mildred, Charles's much-loved and elderly wife. Mildred Covington was of the traditional values. She married at age twenty, had not worked outside the home a day in her life, and everything she did, she did to ensure the comfort of her husband.

Mildred did not understand a woman like C.J. The woman must be at least thirty years old and worked every day. No wonder she did not have a husband. C.J. seemed happy enough, but it wasn't right. The Lord God intended for women to stay at home and look after their menfolk.

"And how are you dear?" Mildred asked C.J. with concern, patting her on the arm.

"Oh me? I'm like a cow in clover, Mildred. Doing just great."

Mildred clucked. Keeping up such a brave face. But with no husband to comfort her...with all this violence ...how could she be alright? Tsk. Tsk.

"But it's Charles here I'm worried about," C.J. continued. "I think he's overdoing things, bringing ladders into work. Do you know why he brought the ladder in on Monday?"

"Oh yes," said Mildred, eager to be helpful. "The leaves were piling up in the gutters on the roof. Charles couldn't bear for that to go on. It can damage the roof, so he tells me."

"I see," said C.J., nodding earnestly. "That is hard work for a man of eighty-seven. Two weeks ago I saw him emptying the trash cans. You know, we have a team of maintenance men who take care of these things."

Mildred pursed her lips. She didn't like to hear her Charles being criticized. But all the same, it sounded like the girl was concerned. "Well, if Charles enjoys these things...it sounds like he is doing the department a favor. Looking after it."

"You are so right, Mildred," said C.J. emphatically. "He is doing us a favor. But, we must think of Charles first. It was just this Monday, after bringing in the ladder, that he had to rest all afternoon at home with you. I don't want him tiring himself unnecessarily."

"Well, now. That's not true. He didn't stop at home on Monday afternoon. I had my crochet group over on Monday. Charles would never stick around for that. He popped in for lunch around noon after he cleaned the leaves off the roof in the morning…it is so handy that we live so close to the department…but then he went right back to work. So you see, I don't think his little odd jobs are a problem."

C.J. looked at Mildred for a moment. "This Monday that just past. The day that Edmund was murdered. Charles wasn't at home all afternoon?"

Mildred wondered if the girl was as bright as they said she was. "No, honey. Charles doesn't crochet. He went back to work."

*****

Mary Beth was standing in line, back straight, buns tight, bosoms out. You never knew when you were going to meet your future husband. She had not seen Professor Daniels yet that evening, but, as her mother said, "It's the money and the ring that matters, not the man providing them."

Mary Beth was scanning the room, looking for other potential life-mates, when Peter Johansson walked by. Like a fly walking into a spider's trap.

"Yoo hoo! Professor Johansson!" Mary Beth called out.

Professor Johansson looked up in surprise. He had little interaction with Mary Beth. He was instinctively afraid of her talon-like nails. Peter nervously ran a hand over his bald head.

"Um. Yes. Miss Sanders, I believe. Can I assist you with anything?"

Mary Beth gave Peter Johansson her most winning smile. "Well, aren't you a gentleman. As a matter of fact, you can. I am standing in this line, waiting to see the body of Professor DeBeyer, and I am feeling a little faint with grief. I was wondering if you would stand with me a while."

Peter Johansson looked at the closed casket, covered in forget-me-nots, and wondered how this girl thought she was going to see the strangled body of Edmund DeBeyer, but didn't comment on this clear breakdown in logic.

"Well, um, of course, yes," he said, coming to stand in the waiting line which hadn't moved at all as Walter was still talking at Lisa. Peter wondered to himself what Walter could possibly say to Edmund's widow. *"I hated your husband with a passion"* or *"Your husband was almost as big a dick as I am."* Somehow, neither seemed appropriate just now.

Peter became aware that Mary Beth was talking to him. Actually, she probably hadn't stopped. Guiltily, he tuned in.

"...so, the police made me aware of the very important role I have in, like, solving the crime. From my desk, I like see so much. I was the one who saw Professor Choi leaving the building when I was away at lunch, and then when I got back from lunch I saw him return. But he didn't come back right when I did. He came back, like, at about two. I also saw Professor Whitmore sitting outside at those silly parking meters doing her so-called research. And I was at my desk the whole time, except when I went to drop off Professor DeBeyer's letters I had typed for him. And that's when I heard the argument."

"An argument, did you say?" asked Peter with interest. He hadn't heard about the argument before.

"Yes. Well, I heard Professor DeBeyer yelling. But the other person must have been Professor Choi. Because that's who they said did it."

"Um, if you don't mind me asking, what did Professor DeBeyer say?" asked Peter.

"Oh, I don't mind you asking, Professor. Professor DeBeyer yelled something like 'You're finished. You're finished.' It was something like that. Anyway... I didn't see you that afternoon. What were you doing while Professor DeBeyer was being killed?"

Peter was taken slightly aback, but realized the inappropriateness of her question, being asked only feet from the widow of the deceased, was not driven by insensitivity or rudeness, but ignorance. "Teaching," he said gently, "I was teaching my undergraduate class."

*****

A rush of rain-cooled night air swept over the mourners as the doors of the church opened swiftly. Jefferson Daniels, obviously running late, rushed into the room. Even now, two days into grieving for his friend and colleague, his face lined with sleepless nights and tears, Jefferson Daniels was by far the most handsome man in the room.

Peter Johansson was aware he had lost his audience. Mary Beth was standing straighter and directing her gaze in the direction of her first choice. "If you'll excuse me," said Peter.

"Huh?" said Mary Beth, not hearing.

Peter, not one to beg for someone's company, bowed ever so slightly as a good-bye and walked away unnoticed by Mary Beth.

*****

Walter, feeling that Lisa had not been listening to him the entire time he had been consoling her with investment advice, saw Peter Johansson walking by and made his escape. "Well, remember, there is always a risk when starting a new business. Do your research before you set your heart on Santa Fe as the location for your new gallery. If you need more advice, come and see me anytime. Now, if you'll excuse me, I see a colleague I must talk with."

Lisa watched Walter retreat with relief. No wonder Edmund had hated the man so much. He really was insufferable. As she caught her breath, the most spectacular-looking woman in hot pink cowboy boots stepped into her line of vision.

"Well, it sure does suck sour eggs we have to meet like this. I'm C.J. Whitmore. I worked with your husband. And I sure am sorry for your loss. I haven't even found a husband, so I won't even pretend to know what it's like to lose one."

"Thank you. For coming, I mean. I'm sure Edmund would have appreciated it."

"Well now, I'm not too sure about that. Your husband and I, we got along like two tom cats in a small barn. Lots of yowling, some scratching, occasional biting. But I respected him. It pains me to say it, but he was a damn fine economist."

Lisa smiled for the first time. "Two tom cats in a small barn, huh. That might describe Edmund with a lot of his colleagues, don't you think?"

C.J. grinned. "I don't like to speak ill of the dead. But of course, it doesn't stop me. By the way, I'd like you to meet my friend Betsy. She teaches some of the courses for the department."

With this, C.J. turned behind her and tapped Betsy on the shoulder, stopping her from telling more stories about her grandchildren to Charles, who was just nodding, smiling and drinking, in blissful, deaf ignorance.

Betsy came up and shook hands with Lisa. "I am so, so sorry my dear. To be so young and without a husband. What a terrible shock."

Lisa turned her tearless blue eyes on Betsy. "That, if nothing else," she said quietly, "is the truth."

THURSDAY

FROM: Walter Scovill
TO: All faculty
SUBJECT: Edmund DeBeyer Memorial
                  Foundation

Dear Colleagues,

Thank you all for your attendance at Professor DeBeyer's funeral service yesterday evening. I think I speak on behalf of the entire department when I say that it was a lugubrious, but fitting tribute to our departed friend.

Now is the time to move forward, and our thoughts must turn to the Edmund DeBeyer Memorial Foundation. This fine institution, granted to us through Edmund's magnanimous generosity, will be housed here in the economics department on the top floor of 40 Knollwood. Its mission will be to further the distinguished research that Edmund began during his lifetime.

At this stage, I am seeking faculty to form a committee. The initial function of this committee will be to recruit a board of directors to ensure the smooth running of the Memorial Foundation.

I am looking forward to hearing from you, expressing your interest in making Edmund's vision a reality.

Walter

*****

FROM: *C.J. Whitmore*
TO: *All faculty*
SUBJECT: *RE: Edmund DeBeyer Memorial*
                            Foundation

Dear Walter,

Thank you for the opportunity to work on dearest Edmund's Memorial Foundation. However, I regret to inform you that I already have a full-time job. In the economics department. At Eaton University. This position requires that I spend 40% of my time teaching, 40% of my time on research, and 20% of my time doing service activities for the university. I am already overloaded on my teaching requirement, picking up Professor DeBeyer's class. If you would like to reduce some of my current service activities, such as the Faculty Handbook Committee or the Student Code of Conduct Committee, then I would gladly serve on the Foundation Committee. Until this occurs, however, my time is fully committed, and as Edmund's Foundation is not strictly University work, I cannot find additional time for it. I am sure, as Department Chair, you appreciate my desire to prioritize faculty work.

Regards,

C.J. Whitmore

*****

It was Thursday morning and C.J. had just finished teaching her graduate econometrics class. She had arrived to class in what she called a rather growly mood, mostly owing to Walter's email, though it certainly hadn't helped that the rain from the night before had left the air heavy with humidity. That was just what she needed today. Frizzy, humidity hair.

C.J. had festered over Walter's email since reading it at eight that morning. Did she want to volunteer for Edmund's Foundation? Does a pack mule want to carry an extra fifty pounds? Sure, she would love to do extra administrative work on top of teaching an extra class. Not. Lord and the Almighty. Edmund was as much of a pain in the patootie dead as he was alive. Sensing her mood, no one in the class had suggested they form a crime fighting unit. Rather, the students had quietly and studiously written notes, silently praying for the class to end before they became the object of C.J.'s wrath.

An hour and twenty minutes of regression analysis hadn't changed C.J.'s outlook. As she strode heavily up to Mary Beth's desk after class, eyes narrowed and lips tightly pursed, Mary Beth didn't think of C.J. as "growly." The phrase that came to Mary Beth's mind was "bitch-witch."

"You know," Mary Beth would often say, "you can tell when a girlfriend is having one of those days. The bitch-witch just oozes out of every enlarged pore."

C.J. grabbed some paperwork from her satchel and slammed it on Mary-Beth's desk. "Mary Beth," she snapped, glaring at the secretary, "these grant papers need to go off to the Contracts Office. ASAP."

Mary Beth took the papers calmly. "You got it, Professor Whitmore. You know, you look a little stressed out today. But you, like, don't have to stress about this. I've got it."

C.J. took a large breath in and exhaled slowly. Inwardly, she admonished herself. Why was she making her bad morning Mary Beth's bad morning? What was wrong with her today? She forced a smile. "Thank you, Mary Beth."

"No. Really. I don't want to be an assistant for life, but I've got this whole assisting thing down. Like Professor Edmund? He had me type up letters for him just before he died. I had to wear the Dictaphone headphones and everything. But," Mary Beth paused, looking sad, "he never got the letters anyway. I still got them here. See?"

Mary Beth swiveled in her chair, took some papers out of a tray on her desk and handed them to C.J. "Do you think they're important? I spent a long time typing them. Should I send them anyway or give them to Professor Scovill?"

C.J. scanned the letters. A selection of refusals... without even pretending regret. Edmund would not be attending two conferences, serving on an editorial board, nor acting as a referee for a journal he frequently published in. (*Really,* thought C.J. dryly, *did the man not know how to use email? Or, for that matter, understand that 'College' stems from 'Collegial?'*) And ...what was this letter to Professor Brustad? C.J. read the letter closely and then looked up at Mary Beth.

"Don't worry about these letters, Mary Beth," C.J. assured the young secretary, with only a slight twinge of her conscience. "They're just boring correspondence to journals and conferences. Why don't I take them and let the people know what has happened with Edmund?"

"Great!" agreed Mary Beth, glad to have some paper shift off her desk.

"By the way, Mary Beth," C.J. asked offhandedly as she was walking away, "I know you saw Stephen going downtown about one o'clock on the day Edmund was murdered. Did you see anyone else out and about that day?"

Mary Beth, eager to keep Professor Whitmore in her improved humor, was glad the question was so easy. "I know! It's like, OMG! Can you believe I saw a murderer? I was telling my mother last night, I am so lucky he didn't kill me.

"I also saw Jefferson," Mary Beth added, trying to be as helpful as she could be. "At ten past one. Here. In the department."

"Ten past one?" asked C.J. questioningly.

"Oh. No. Maybe that's not right. My new watch is so confusing. Maybe it was when the big hand was at the ten. That's not the same time, is it?"

"Not exactly," said C.J. slowly. Not for the first time, C.J. wondered what it was like to have an I.Q. below 175. She didn't see a lot of difference between Mary Beth's intelligence and that of her cat.

"Well, I saw him at the end of his run," said Mary Beth, trying to clear up the confusion. "He's a really good runner. But, it was before the seminar, which started at two. And it was before I saw that graduate student, what's her name…Antiga…no, that's not right …well, whatever. She left here crying her eyes out something awful just before two. I guess economics isn't, like, happy, smiley faces all the time."

"Thanks for your help today, Mary Beth," said C.J., as she left the secretary's office looking thoughtful.

*****

FROM: Charles Covington III
TO: All faculty
SUBJECT: RE: Edmund DeBeyer Memorial
Foundation

Walter,

I never liked the bugger. I'm not serving on any committee to help his egotistical, self-serving foundation. I think it is a travesty the thing is getting precious department space.

You can absolutely count on me to give you zero support on this.

Charles Covington III
*****

Betsy recognized the young woman from the economics department. The girl looked sad. No, not sad. Worried. It had been many years since Betsy Williams had been a young, slender graduate student. So long, that only Charles Covington III had been in the department when Betsy was studying for her Ph.D. at Eaton University. But Betsy still remembered the life of a graduate student. There had been so much stress and so many expectations.

Betsy picked up her coffee order and eased her large frame next to the young girl. "Do you mind if I share the table?"

Annika looked up, startled. "Oh. No, no. No. I don't mind." Politeness dictated her answer, though her body language indicated she would much rather not share her table with this hulking mass of cellulite that was expanding and perspiring in the most unflattering manner due to the humidity.

Betsy pushed the conversation. "My name is Betsy Williams. I teach for the econ department."

"Oh. You are a professor?" Annika's tone changed immediately. Good-bye melancholy loner. Hello friendly professional. This woman could be the reference that landed the job that would start her career. "I am Annika Jonsdottir. I am a graduate student for econ."

"Nice to meet you Annika. But no, I'm not a professor. I'm an adjunct instructor. I just teach classes."

"Oh. Okay." The slump was beginning to return to the young woman's shoulders. There was no need to fake cheer and enthusiasm for an adjunct. An adjunct could do nothing for her.

"Yes. It is okay. I like my job." Betsy thought it was good to start this message early with graduate students. Too often, she had seen them take the jobs that they were expected to take, rather than the ones they wanted. "But are you okay? I couldn't help noticing you looked a little worried or upset."

Annika shook her head and looked intently at her cup of coffee.

"Yoo-hoo, Betsy!" A loud call echoed across the coffee shop.

Both Betsy and Annika looked up and saw C.J. across the room, waving at Betsy.

Betsy turned to Annika. "Well, obviously and not very quietly, my friend has arrived. But if you ever need to talk, you can find me. I was a graduate student myself once. I know if you don't learn to lever the expectations, they can crush you."

Betsy hefted herself out of the chair and patted Annika on the arm. As she walked away, tears began to slide down Annika's cheeks.

*****

"That poor girl," Betsy said to C.J. "She is not coping. What are you doing to those dear graduate students?"

C.J. glanced over Betsy's shoulder to look at Annika, but the young girl was packing up and leaving. Troubled souls weren't C.J.'s strong suit. "I don't know what's going on. Boy troubles maybe? I think Jose stood her up last week. But really, Betsy, we have bigger issues to worry about right now."

"Of course. Of course. How is your lemon hunt going?"

"Well, as sure as chickens come from eggs, I know Stephen is not the lemon. Maybe instead," C.J. paused, searching for the right words, "a slightly bruised apple. But that is all."

"So how do you know for certain he didn't do it?" asked Betsy. "There must be a reason he's sitting in Elm Grove City Jail at this very moment."

"Well," hesitated C.J., "that's a little awkward. The bruise on Stephen's apple is his alibi and that is why he won't mention it. I'm going to visit the boy this afternoon to see if I can't talk some sense into him."

Betsy sipped her coffee through pursed lips. Really, C.J. could be so infuriating. If she knew something, why didn't she just come out and say it? Betsy's lengthy marriage had given her many years practice in ignoring those who were frustrating her, so she placed her coffee cup down gently and got out her latest project. Today, she was crocheting a baby blanket for grandchild number seventeen, expected in only four months.

Betsy was busy stitching her foundation chain, oblivious to those around her, muttering *thirty-one, thirty-two, thirty-three, thirty-four*...when something C.J. said caused her to look up and lose count.

"...so I was thinking that you might be right, and Jefferson might be the murderer," concluded C.J.

"What?" asked Betsy blankly, her crochet hook hanging limply in one hand, and the yarn collapsed in her lap like a disheartened snake.

"Bet-sy Will-iams," C.J. elongated her friend's name in exasperation. Her growly mood of the morning was clearly not completely eradicated. "I just explained why I thought Jefferson could have murdered Edmund."

"But, but," stammered Betsy, "the other day, I didn't really think that was true. It was just that on all the T.V. shows, it's always the least likely person. Why would Jefferson kill Edmund?"

"Revenge. Mary Beth showed me a letter today she had to type for Edmund. Here, read it for yourself." C.J. pulled the letter to Professor Brustad out of her satchel. "I would say Edmund was a swine, but I actually like pigs."

Betsy looked over the letter, still looking confused.

"Do you realize what this means? Edmund was ruining Jefferson's reputation…saying all their joint work was really Edmund's work. Please. Edmund had been riding Jefferson's coat tails for years. I think it was because the Nobel (and its more than one million dollars in prize money) was in the offing. Edmund didn't want to share the glory or the cash."

"But to kill? Over a letter?"

"This isn't just a letter, Betsy. This is a career. And a brilliant, very public one at that."

Betsy picked up her crocheting again. She had completely lost count of the number of stitches in the chain and felt too befuddled to recount them. This poor grandchild was going to have some very uneven squares in his or her blanket. "So…how do you think Jefferson killed Edmund?" asked Betsy as she tried to come to terms with the new theory.

"Well, that is interesting," said C.J. "The police say the time of death was after one and before two. So Edmund was alive at noon when Jefferson says he left for his run. And Jefferson says he ran around campus twice. When Jeffie came into seminar at two, he was out of breath and in running clothes, which backs up his story. I think, if he is our lemon, the highest probability event is that Jefferson stopped off in the econ building between laps, went up to Edmund's office and strangled him."

"He could have," said Betsy uncertainly, "but surely someone would have seen him."

"I'm not convinced that someone didn't. Mary Beth, God love her for trying to wear an analog watch, is very confused about the time she saw Jefferson that afternoon. First, it was ten past one. Then, it was ten to two. If she did in fact see him at ten past one, he could have ducked up to Edmund's office, been the person that Edmund argued with, killed him, and then continued on with his run. Jefferson sure had the motive to kill Edmund."

Betsy looked down at the trapezoidal, baby-blue shape she had crocheted and frowned. "Well, I think you're wrong. I really like Jefferson, and he's been really upset that Edmund died. You can't fake that. I don't think he could be our lemon."

*****

FROM: *Peter Johansson*
TO: *All faculty*
SUBJECT: *RE: Edmund DeBeyer Memorial*
              Foundation

Walter,

I appreciate the importance of the DeBeyer Foundation project to the faculty and the University. I look forward to being able to contribute my time and expertise at some stage in the future. However, at the moment, my time is committed with my role as Chair of the Hiring Committee. I am sure you understand.

Peter

*****

C.J. sat on the grey plastic bucket chair in the visitors' room of the Elm Grove City Jail, anxiously tapping a tuneless song with the heels of her cowboy boots. Really. Did PETA ever visit jails? They were so against cattle ranches, but the local jail had by-passed their attention? This was inhumane. Everything was so grey, so sterile. Not to mention invasive.

Five minutes earlier, C.J. had held her arms out in a giant T shape, allowing a guard to wand, scan or pat down every possible body part that could possibly carry contraband. The guards had been very clear at the reception desk. No guns. No knives. No food. No cell phones. No letters. No hard cover books. No pens. No pencils. C.J. got the message. In a jail, anything was a potential weapon.

Now, cleared of being a smuggler, C.J. sat uncomfortable and irritated. Her growly mood of earlier was back with a vengeance. She continued to tap out a rhythm with her shoes, which only served to annoy her further. What was that song she was tip-tapping with her feet? The theme to M*A*S*H? No, that wasn't it, though it would have been apt.

Just then, another guard showed Stephen into the room, bringing an end to C.J.'s game of "guess this tune." Dressed in an orange jumpsuit, Stephen looked small, disheveled, and in need of a long, hot shower.

C.J. looked at the man, exasperated. "What did you get your Ph.D. in? Economics, or stupidity?"

Stephen looked back, rather stunned by this unexpected attack.

C.J. continued. If she could break a temperamental stallion, she could sure handle the tangerine hamster sitting before her. "I know where you were the hour before Edmund's death. You understand me? And it wasn't killing Edmund."

"You can't know," said Stephen quietly.

"Oh, get over yourself Stephen. I don't know what weird, ritualistic honor code you are trying to respect, but the time for that has passed. I know and unless you want to go to jail for the murder of Edmund, which, by the way, will let a murderer roam free, a whole lot of other people need to know. So tell your lawyer or I will." C.J. paused and took in a deep breath.

Really. People. More proof that they lacked rationality. In the cute, little model of the used car market, no one was trying to make his good car look like crap. But here was Stephen, letting himself look like the lemon. Who knew what everyone else was doing?

*****

FROM: Walter Scovill
TO: All faculty
SUBJECT: Edmund DeBeyer Memorial
Foundation, AGAIN

Dear Colleagues,

I feel I wasn't clear in my first email as not a single person has volunteered to assist with the Edmund DeBeyer Memorial Foundation.

I need three faculty members working on this project ASAP. If I don't have three volunteers by eight tomorrow morning, I will be informing three lucky faculty members that they will have the honor.

Walter

*****

FROM: Jefferson Daniels
TO: All faculty
SUBJECT: RE: Edmund DeBeyer Memorial
Foundation, AGAIN

Dear Walter,

I guess this is as good a time as any to mention that I submitted my resignation to the Dean of Arts and Sciences today. Therefore, while I would love to be one of the three lucky faculty members chosen for your committee, at the end of this semester, I will be leaving Eaton University. Before you start calling around, I am not going to Harvard or Princeton. I am moving to New Mexico to become an alpaca farmer. I have never actually cared for the discipline of economics. It is rather dull, especially in large quantities, don't you find?

Jefferson

*****

C.J. rang Betsy as soon as she read Jefferson's email. She could hear Betsy's husband and his friends in the background, yelling wildly.

"Sorry about the noise," apologized Betsy. "It's only preseason football, but New England is down by three."

C.J. understood football. Her daddy had been a big football fan. So, her Sundays had been spent 'watching and learning the game,' which involved little more than sitting around as her father yelled plays at the T.V. set and screamed obscenities when the coach of the Dallas Cowboys didn't listen to the advice that he couldn't possibly hear. What was not to love about the game? "Not a problem. Have you got time to talk?"

"Sure thing. Hold on a moment. I'm going to move somewhere quieter."

C.J. hung on and listened as Betsy wheezed her way up the stairs. Eventually, the sounds of the football game died away, and Betsy's breathing returned to normal.

"So," said Betsy, "I always like to talk to you, but you don't normally call at ten on a Thursday night. Anything the matter?"

"You, my friend, are not going to believe the news I have."

"Try me."

"Jefferson Daniels, the man I thought had murdered Edmund because Edmund was trashing his professional reputation, just resigned and is going to be an alpaca farmer in New Mexico!"

"No!"

"Yes!"

"No!"

"I'm forwarding you the email as we speak, in case it didn't get sent to the adjuncts."

"Wait. I'm logging on to my email. Wait. Wait. Oh my goodness. That poor man. Imagine being an economics professor if you didn't like economics. That is rather tragic. Well, it doesn't seem likely he cared much about Edmund's letter writing campaign if he was planning on quitting. That lemon's gone."

"I know. But still..."

"But still what?"

"Nothing. What if Jefferson's cracking up? What if Jefferson just can't handle academic life without Edmund? You see it in the barn sometimes. You have a cow and a goat that were raised together. The cow dies, and the goat dies heartbroken within weeks. Jefferson could be the goat."

Betsy hummed into the phone. Jefferson didn't strike her as a goat. The man had managed to scrabble from the projects to Eaton University. If he didn't fall apart during that process, she didn't think Edmund's dying was going to do it. "I'm not sure. But there must be some reason he wants alpacas instead of economics."

"You're right. I'm going to talk to Walter tomorrow. I'll make sure he gives Jefferson leave without pay. So Jeffie can change his mind after a year of shoveling alpaca poo. He doesn't know what a ranch is like. I don't think it's the solution he is looking for."

*****

It was just after ten on Thursday night when Stephen finally broke down and confessed the existence of an alibi. It wasn't clear whether it was the fact C.J. was going to tell anyway, the bedbugs were enjoying the all-you-can-eat buffet at his feet and ankles each night, or the small issue that he was looking at serving life in jail for a crime he didn't commit, that caused Stephen to change his mind.

When Stephen told his lawyer where he actually was in the hour leading up to the discovery of Edmund's body, the man snorted coffee out his nose.

"No effing way! Please tell me you weren't going to sizzle in the electric chair for this."

Stephen looked back coldly. It was good that one of them had ethical standards. And knew the law. There was no death penalty in Connecticut any more.

"No. Seriously, man. That's where you were?"

Stephen nodded.

"How many people were there?"

Stephen looked uncomfortable. He didn't want to say.

"Oh. Jesus and his Virgin Mother. I am not asking for their socials. Just how many?"

"Five, including me," said Stephen.

Stephen's lawyer let a squirt of tobacco juice fly from the side of one cheek. Most of his clients invented alibis. They sure didn't keep them hidden. Professors. They pulled the craziest crap this side of the Mississippi. What a bunch of weirdos.

"Well, bud. We'll need a name."

Stephen shook his head.

The lawyer breathed in deeply. "Do I need to explain how this works to you, boy? Your alibis are as valuable as an ice cube in Hell unless they are actual people with actual names who talk to actual district attorneys."

Just over an hour later Stephen, head in his hands, gave a name.

FRIDAY

FROM: Walter Scovill
TO: All faculty
SUBJECT: Edmund DeBeyer Memorial
Foundation, YET AGAIN

Dear Colleagues,

Yesterday, I received two offers of assistance for the Edmund DeBeyer Memorial Foundation. Two.
So today I have the pleasure of appointing the third committee member.
It is C.J. Whitmore.

Walter

*****

When Jose had arrived at Eaton University, two years before, Walter had made the situation clear. He, Walter, had been responsible for Jose's acceptance into this world class educational institution. This esteemed bastion of higher learning. This portal to a brighter future. Jose had been given a scholarship. He didn't have to pay a single penny for this wonderful education. In fact, Eaton University was going to pay Jose a stipend. Not a fortune, but enough to live on.

"The only wrinkle in this situation," Walter had said, his hand stroking his chin as he perched on his desk looking down at Jose, who sat in the chair in front of him, "the little wrinkle is that you would not have been accepted but for me. You would not have these opportunities, this money, this gateway to the world beyond."

Jose had watched Walter with steady eyes. Walter had thought he was being very smooth, but Jose had lived on the streets of Tijuana since he was orphaned at age six. He had seen everything. He had done most things. This man was pathetic.

"So, Jose," Walter continued, with a greasy smile, "the way I see it is that you will need to...pay me some student fees, as it were. To make sure I am happy and don't change my mind about your application."

"You want money?" asked Jose, even though he knew money wasn't the issue here.

"No, no. I don't want your money. I have plenty, and you have so little."

"Oh," said Jose. He wasn't going to make this easy for Walter.

The two men sat across from each other in silence.

"You want the sex?" Jose finally asked in a tired voice. It seems it was always the sex. It did not matter how rich or poor men were or what nationality, they always wanted the sex.

Walter blanched. "No! No. No," he hastened to clear up this issue right away. "I don't like...um...I am not ...um...attracted to men...not that there is anything wrong with that."

Walter tried to regain his composure. He never said no to an eager young undergraduate, but they were always female students. He thought that was obvious. "Jose. I am expecting you to...exchange your... laboring skills...for your place in the graduate school at Eaton University. A simple economic transaction. You need an education. I need a...houseboy. Understand?"

Jose nodded. He understood. Slavery wasn't the right term, as he was sure it would end when he graduated. Indentured servitude seemed a better definition. A contract to be at Walter's beck and call for the duration of his Ph.D.

Which was why this Friday, Jose responded to Walter's summons and arrived at his office just before eight-thirty.

Surprisingly, Jose did not despise Walter. If Jose needed to shine Walter's shoes, rake his leaves and polish his car so he could stay at Eaton University, then he could pay that price. Jose viewed Walter as he had every man that he serviced on the streets of Tijuana. Something to step on as he worked his way up the ladder of success. One did not despise a rock, a dog turd, the ground beneath his feet. In Jose's mind, this was what these men were.

This particular Friday, Walter was enjoying his morning shoe shine. Jose was wearing a leather shoe shining apron and a blue and white striped cap. Walter was reclining in his leather office chair, and Jose was kneeling before him. Walter's right leg was stretched out and his right foot was resting on Jose's apron-covered leg. Jose was working up a sweat polishing Walter's right shoe, rubbing it vigorously with a polishing cloth.

Walter, always one to enjoy a position of power, was yelling instructions at Jose.

"More polish on the toe!"

"Rub harder, boy!"

"Make 'em shine boy. Make 'em shine."

Somewhere in the midst of Walter's commands, an outraged C.J., ready to do battle over her appointment to the Edmund DeBeyer Memorial Foundation, flung open the door.

Silence filled the room. With a horrified look, C.J. looked from Walter to Jose and back to Walter again. Walter remained frozen in position, right leg outstretched. Jose turned his head away. It was one thing to work for Professor Scovill. It was another for Professor Whitmore, whom he respected greatly, to know. What could he say? He wasn't smart enough to earn his place at Eaton University on his own merits.

"Walter. We need to talk. About this Memorial Committee business. And about Jefferson. But clearly now is not the time. Send me an email when you are not …" C.J. stumbled to find the right word. Walter wasn't busy, as he wasn't doing any work himself. To say "exploiting people" seemed a tad aggressive. C.J. just left the sentence unfinished. "And Jose," Jose looked up, his face flaming red. "Don't forget you are taking recitation section at nine today."

*****

Stephen Choi's lawyer had earned his hefty retainer by working through the night to confirm Stephen's alibi and secure his release. While this news was personally exciting to Mr. Choi, in the view of the general public, an innocent person is just like every other innocent person. Boring. Therefore, Stephen Choi was released from jail at ten o'clock on Friday morning without having a single photo taken or question asked of him by the vigilant media. However, had anyone bothered to ask what his time in jail had been like, Stephen would have told them the startling truth. He had learned more economics during his brief incarceration than in the five years of his doctoral education.

Ramen was the basic currency of the jail. Coffee was a gold coin. A hair cut could be bought for three packs of ramen, unless the guy who did the haircuts was running low on food. Then the price dropped to just one ramen. Or even a half, depending on how long it was to commissary day and how desperate the guy was for non-prison food. Protection during a shower…five ramen. A smuggled cell phone…a cup of coffee. There was no surplus in a jail economy. Everything could be used for something. A ball point pen? Contraband but excellent for tattoos. A sheet of paper? Depends on how much you liked the guy.

It was somewhat of a waste that Stephen had finally gleaned such a deep understanding of economics, as what Stephen was not going back to, at least for now, was his job. The Dean of Arts and Sciences had dropped by the jail earlier that morning, as soon as he had been made aware of Stephen's innocence and impending release.

"Stephen," the Dean had begun with a strong handshake and a politician's smile. Never a sign of good news. "I, we, all of the university are so pleased to hear that your innocence had been proven."

Stephen nodded. The Dean didn't actually look that thrilled. Stephen understood. If you were going to have a murdering professor, a junior professor already on the way out was optimal. Now that Stephen was innocent, who was it?

"But we need to discuss your return date."

"I rather thought that would be today, sir."

"Yes, yes. I appreciate your good intentions. But we must think of the university first. There are some parents, some…influential parents…who would prefer not to have…someone…arrested for murder…on the campus with their precious babies."

Stephen opened his mouth to object. It wasn't even like he was teaching any classes this semester.

"Now Stephen, you and I know such an attitude is ridiculous. You are, after all, not a proven murderer. But we must cater to the client. So take a sabbatical. The less time you are in the department in the next few days, or even…weeks, the better. Am I clear?"

Stephen understood perfectly. A man was innocent until proven guilty or condemned by wealthy Eaton donors.

So now, as he stood at the curb waiting, it was not to go back to work. But rather, it was for a taxi to take him to the airport. If Eaton University was going to run him out of town, then he was going to enjoy some time with his much-ignored girlfriend. There was going to be something good that came of all this.

*****

The Eaton University administration was right to be unhappy about Stephen's release. Stephen's innocence heralded the return of an unwelcome spotlight back on Eaton's campus. A spotlight, the President thought bitterly, that could only slow the growth of the endowment. The police returned, somewhat like stubborn bathroom mold, questioning faculty and students.

"Where were you exactly on the day Edmund was murdered?"

"Can anyone corroborate that?"

"Talk us through the day in question just one more time."

The media, singularly uninterested in Stephen's innocence, re-camped their reporters on the most magnificent street in America in the hopes of capturing the bigger story. Who was the murderer? Would he strike again?

Charles Covington was in his office at 41 Knollwood, being interviewed by two rather unhappy and paunchy police officers, aged in their late thirties. At the station that morning, the cases on the board were the drive-by shooting of a fifteen-year-old boy, a drug overdose death of a thirty-two-year-old mother of five, and the Edmund DeBeyer murder case. The boys in blue drew straws to see who got to work on what. The gentlemen in Charles's office drew the short straw.

Charles was glaring across his desk at the two officers, wondering how old they were. Fifteen, sixteen? They certainly looked like children. Why were they so interested in him? He didn't kill that annoying termite of a man.

"Thank you for taking the time to meet with us again, Professor Covington."

Police officers were always so polite, Charles thought churlishly. Charles ran his fingers through his white hair, causing it to stand up at an even more startling angle than usual. He just grunted a response to their comment.

"We are interested in what you did after lunch on the Monday that Edmund DeBeyer was killed."

"I told you already. I stopped at home and spent the afternoon with Mildred."

"Yes. We realize that is what you said. But someone at the funeral overheard Mildred saying you went back to work that afternoon. So you can see our dilemma. Where exactly were you, Professor Covington? At home or at work?"

Charles huffed into his mustache. A man has no privacy these days. He couldn't even walk to work without that C.J. gal stopping him to ask him how he was feeling. How did she think he was feeling? He was eighty-seven years old. He was hardly a new model. A few things were rusty and breaking down. But try getting a washing machine or one of those fancy new Apple pad things to last 87 years. Hah! Not likely.

But again, all these questions. Questions, questions, questions. What was it now? Where was he exactly the afternoon Edmund died? "None of your damn business," Charles answered gruffly.

"Sir…" began one of the policemen. He did not get paid enough for this. The drug overdose would have been so much easier. It was very unlikely this elderly man strangled his workmate. But he did need an answer.

"That's Professor to you, you whippersnapper. And I think our time is up. I have to teach class." With this, Charles went and held open the door, and the two men, needing to rethink their strategy of dealing with Charles, left meekly. Charles, who did not teach class that day, eased himself back into his desk chair to think. What was the best thing to do?

*****

While C.J. did not teach class on Fridays, Jose was in charge of the recitation sections for her undergraduate class, and she was concerned he might not show. So she decided to pop in on the nine a.m. class that morning. Despite having their cell phones surgically attached to their bodies, her students seemed to have terrible trouble telling time. At nine o'clock, C.J. and a very quiet Jose had little more than half the recitation section sitting before them in the room. C.J. just smiled at those who were on time and said, "Actions speak much louder than words, don't ya'll think?"

The students arriving later were surprised to find the door to the room locked and a note placed up. "Hope you can join us next class. It begins at nine."

Having just re-enacted the shaking of the door handle, the bemused faces peering in the little glass square in the door, and the terrified faces of those inside the room for the benefit of Betsy over their morning coffee, C.J. paused for breath. "If I'm perfectly honest, I prefer a smaller class size. Can I start locking the door earlier and earlier?"

Betsy, her entire girth shaking with laughter, just shook her head. "Oh Lord. Only you would lock them out." Today, Betsy was knitting a pink and purple striped scarf and hat for her ten year old granddaughter. Once the laughter settled down, the sound of the needles clicking resumed.

"Why not? I hate having them walk in after class has started. But I tell you, it is easier to get the cows to come in for milking than get those students into a lecture hall on time. Do their parents know how they behave?"

"I hope not. Because then they would stop paying, and you and I would be out of a job."

"Depressing. But I did talk to that one student. That girl I thought I recognized on the first day. Her economics knowledge is far superior to the rest of the class. So I complimented her after class today, and she said 'Well, I guess I am my father's daughter,' like that would mean something. But I looked up her last name, and it's Wilson. I don't know any famous Wilson economists, do you? I thought they were tennis racquet makers."

Betsy shook her head. "No. I can't think of any. But you know the Eaton students. They all think they are much more famous than they are."

"Isn't that the truth? Hey, did I tell you I talked to Stephen?" C.J. took a long sip of her large hazelnut latte, extra cream and cinnamon sprinkled on top. Since she had started teaching the extra class, her coffee orders had become even more extravagant as a reward. Just like giving a dog a biscuit for good behavior.

"How is that poor boy doing?"

"Well, I don't think you bounce back from being falsely accused of being a murderer. He's spending some time with his girlfriend at Berkeley."

"Stephen has a girlfriend?" Betsy's knitting stopped as she looked up in surprise.

"Right. I didn't know either. But apparently, yes. A grad student in chemistry."

"Huh." Betsy started knitting again in earnest. Her lap was a pink and purple sea of fluffy wool.

"So, I've been thinking about Stephen getting released. Of course, it is good news for Stephen, but unfortunately, it is rather bad news for the rest of us."

"How do you figure? I thought you liked Stephen."

"No, no. That's not it. What I mean is that, well, because Stephen didn't kill Edmund, and I never thought he did, there is still a murderer working alongside us every day. And now the murderer knows that we know he's still out there."

"Oh, yes. I see, I think. Well, if this was *Law and Order*, the murderer would do something really soon to give himself away. Like try and go back to the scene of the crime, or kill someone else."

"Comforting, Betsy. Very comforting."

*****

At a little after eleven-thirty, Betsy left Wallaby's and walked right by Walter Scovill. She lowered her head and gave a respectful nod. Walter was, after all, her boss.

Walter groaned inwardly. She knew! That cowhand they had somehow hired had told. He could tell. Betsy Williams, of all people, was looking down at him. It was intolerable. He, Walter, hadn't done anything wrong. It was a fair market exchange. Labor for education. It was not to be stood for. He would take care of C.J. Whitmore. Now.

Walter stormed back to the department and into the faculty lounge. Jefferson was sitting in an over-stuffed leather chair, sipping his smoothie. Opposite him sat Peter, drinking his coffee and eating a chocolate glazed. Charles, looking very distracted, was standing by the coffee machine, stirring his Styrofoam cup of coffee endlessly. A smattering of the 41 and 43 Knollwood crowd was chattering at the back of the room. Stephen Choi of course wasn't there. Walter had reluctantly agreed he could take some time off work, but had agreed only because he had already denied Stephen tenure. And, of course, because the Dean had called and told him that it would be better if Stephen wasn't around. But really, how soft was the man? So he spent a few days in jail for a crime he didn't commit. Buck up and get back to work.

Walter bounced into the room, red in the face. Startled, everyone looked up. Walter looked around, gradually realizing he wouldn't find his target there. Of course. C.J. didn't come to faculty coffee anymore. They hadn't seen her there since the day she got tenure. God only knew what her problem was. Walter's eyes eventually settled on Jefferson.

Jefferson gave the man an amused smile. "What's up, Walter? Here to give me my forty acres and mule and send me on my way to Sante Fe?"

Jefferson chuckled at his little joke. A little black humor was always fun in a white department. He had been expecting the wrath of Walter since he announced his resignation, but not so publicly. But the effect on Walter was not what Jefferson expected.

"God! I will not stand for this. You understand me? Edmund tried the power play, and I crushed him like a bug. You don't want to test me boy."

With this startling statement, Walter flounced out of the faculty lounge, leaving his colleagues open-mouthed.

*****

Jefferson was pacing in C.J.'s office two hours later.

"Do you think we need to tell the police?"

C.J., sitting in her desk chair, watched the nervous energy that was Jefferson Daniels. No wonder the man published ten articles a year and ran a few marathons on the side. He clearly had an excess of fuel to burn. Was that a medical condition? Something with the thyroid? She couldn't remember.

C.J. leaned back in her chair, pink cowboy boots slung up on the desk. "Tell me again. What exactly did he say?"

Jefferson paused his pacing and faced C.J. "He wasn't going to stand for it. And I shouldn't test him. And that Edmund had tried the power play and had been squashed like a bug."

Jefferson resumed his figure eights of C.J.'s red and yellow kachina-doll-themed area rug.

C.J. pursed her lips, moving them from side to side. "What did you say right before that?"

Jefferson didn't stop walking to answer C.J. this time. "Walter looked upset. I just joked about how upset he was looking."

"What exactly did you say?"

"Oh, I don't know," Jefferson stopped to think. He replayed the scene in the lounge in his mind and then looked at C.J. "I think I said something about him paying me my forty acres and a mule. I admit, it was not in great taste. But as the only African-American on the faculty, I like to draw attention to the fact from time to time. I admit it. You know what I am talking about, Miss-Only-Tenured-Female."

C.J. suppressed a smile, but Jefferson saw it.

"What? What did I say?"

"Nothing important. Try not to worry too much about Walter. I really don't think he is going to kill you." But as C.J. said this, she wondered. Walter had a temper, and it seemed to flare when he was provoked. Did Edmund provoke Walter as well?

*****

Jefferson had gone, and C.J. was left in the peace of her office. She was sifting through her email. Therese in accounting was organizing a cookie swap for the holidays. She knew it was early, but sign up now! C.J. hit delete. What an idea. Baking dozens of your favorite cookies, then giving them away, and taking home plates of cookies that you would only eat if trapped in your house for the fifth day without food. It made no sense at all to her as an economist. Trading something good for something crappy.

Norm from the safety department was alerting them to a fire drill on Friday at seven a.m. C.J. hit delete. Good job, Norm. There would be no one there Friday at seven. Perfect for convenience, a little less useful for safety.

Janet from payroll wanted everyone to know that Thursday was pay day. C.J. just rolled her eyes. Janet, darling, do you think people don't know that? You could skip that email…we will flood your inbox if, for some reason, we don't get paid. Trust me. Delete.

Then there was a selection of emails informing C.J. of exciting training opportunities using smartboards, clickers and other technologies in the classroom. About ten emails announced either has-beens or soon-to-be-someones speaking around campus. One email informed faculty where they could find the menu for various eateries on campus. Two promised thrilling upcoming Fall-fest events that should not be missed.

DELETE…DELETE…DELETE

When C.J. had first arrived at Eaton University, she had changed her email settings to direct all such emails into her spam folder. She had been enjoying the freedom from this daily update of the frivolous and mundane until the secretary from the Dean's office called one day, sounding rather annoyed.

"The Dean has emailed you eleven times. He expects a response."

"The Dean has emailed? I haven't gotten an email from the Dean."

After a few minutes of searching through her spam folder and a very long and sincere apology from C.J., the problem was solved. C.J. was told curtly by the Dean, who did not find the situation amusing, to change her spam filter.

Consequently, C.J. now spent fifteen minutes every day deleting requests to join the bowling team or attend pumpkin carving competitions. With this chore done for the day, C.J. remembered Jose, looking so awkward at the recitation. She didn't want to leave things that way.

FROM: C.J. Whitmore
TO: Jose Grimaldo
SUBJECT: Touching base

Jose,

I wanted to have a quick chat. There is some grading coming up that you will need to do for the undergraduate class. Also, I wanted to check in, to see how things are. Can you stop by my office?

Professor Whitmore

Jose must have been sitting at his computer, not surprising for a graduate student, as C.J. got a response right back.

FROM: Jose Grimaldo
TO: C.J. Whitmore
SUBJECT: RE: Touching base

Professor Whitmore,

Of course. How about Monday after Econ 101? Grading for Econ 101...always fun.

As for checking in, everything is great with me. Thanks for asking.

Jose

C.J. read Jose's email and thought wryly, *'Everything is great.' Really my friend? 1 just saw you on your knees, polishing the shoes oj the Chair oj the department. I'm not sure 1 would call that great. Whether you want to or not, you and 1 will chat today.*

*****

C.J. was just pressing send on her reply to Jose when there was a knock on her office door. It was a timid knock. Not recognizable as any of her colleagues. C.J. often thought that professors had a mistaken reputation of being soft, gentle and kind, locked away in their ivory towers. C.J. had never met a more cut-throat group of professionals, scrabbling up the career ladder by eating the young of those below them. Such men did not knock softly.

However, a student, still awed by the environment, might be hesitant to disturb her. Damn. It wasn't her office hours, and she didn't want to deal with a student. An undergraduate was going to ask questions a hedgehog could answer, and graduate students always had other issues. They were stressed. They were in love. They needed to fly home to Yugoslavia to visit a dying grandmother. Did she look like a counselor?

C.J. scowled at the door. With all the extra faculty meetings, funerals and classes, C.J.'s social tolerance was maxed out. She did not want to speak to another person, help another person, or comfort another person. Period. "Come in," C.J. called half-heartedly. If she was quiet enough, the student would go away, and her conscience would be satisfied that she hadn't actually ignored him or her.

The door opened slightly. "Hello?" an old and shaky voice asked questioningly. "Hello? Professor Whitmore? Are you there?"

"Mildred?" C.J. called out questioningly. C.J. rarely saw Charles's elderly wife in the department.

"Yes. It's me. Mildred." The relief in the old woman's voice was palpable. "Can I come in Professor Whitmore?"

"For goodness sake, of course. Don't be collecting dust out there in the hallway," C.J. said with a cheer she did not feel. "Now, forget this Professor Whitmore business. The name's C.J. Always has been." C.J. looked closely at Mildred. The old lady, a virtual botanical garden in a pink and orange flowered dress complemented with a white hat banded in daisies, had stepped cautiously into her office and was trembling ever so slightly, her head bowed.

"Mildred, take a seat," C.J. encouraged. A Texan lifetime of being polite to her elders kicked in and overrode her real desire to throw the old lady out her window. "It is always a pleasure to see you."

Mildred sat down obediently. "I hope it is alright I came to see you. I didn't know who else to turn to. Certainly not that Professor Scovill." Mildred almost spat out Walter's name. C.J. guessed that Charles was very open about his thoughts on certain faculty members when at home.

"Of course it's okay. I glad you did," C.J. lied. "Is there something in particular that is worrying you Mildred?"

Mildred took a deep breath, dabbed her eyes with a lace handkerchief embroidered with roses, and then broke down into uncontrolled sobs. "It's Charlie. And this stupid murder. Charlie has just gone and confessed that he murdered Edmund."

*****

Walter Scovill sighed impatiently when Charles Covington III called from the Elm Grove Police Station.

"Ah, is that you, Walter?"

"Of course it's me. You rang my office at three in the afternoon. Whom did you think would answer? Kermit the Frog? What do you want?"

"A frog? No. I can't say I was expecting a frog. How strange you would think that. Are you feeling alright, Walter?"

Walter exhaled audibly. "What is it you want Charles?"

"Oh yes. Sorry. Silly me, getting distracted with all this amphibian nonsense. I just thought I should let you know that I, well, I just confessed to murdering Edmund."

Walter was silent. He must have misheard the old boy. Did he just say he murdered Edmund? "Sorry, Charles, I couldn't hear what you just said. Could you repeat it?"

"I said," yelled Charles, thinking the connection must be bad, "I KILLED EDMUND!"

Walter sat back in his desk chair, silent. Not the person he would have picked. Walter had thought Stephen was a likely candidate. Being Asian and all. All that Samurai warrior crap and karate chop sui. Really, a very violent people the Orientals. And if not Stephen, then C.J. was surely a shoe-in. With those hormones and all. But Charles?

"Walter, are you still there?"

"Oh, yes, of course, Charles. Sorry to hear that. Thanks for letting me know." And without further comment, Professor Walter Scovill hung up the phone.

*****

"Of course it's your problem," said Betsy, admonishing C.J. as she recounted her incident with Mildred over a rare, late afternoon coffee. But when C.J. had called Betsy with the news of Charles's confession, the two women had decided they wanted to talk it over in person. "Really C.J., I think you have been spending too much time around Walter. Do you honestly think Charles Covington murdered Edmund DeBeyer?"

"Well, he says he did it. Charles walked into the Elm Grove Police Station with a very convincing story. How he left home after lunch. Mildred had been worried that the petition to remove Charles from the faculty would be successful, and Charles had been in a fury that Edmund had upset Mildred. He came back to the department to work off his bad mood by cleaning gutters. But, as he was climbing the ladder, he saw Edmund through the window. The two men got into an argument. Charles ended up in Edmund's office, and the argument ended with Charles strangling Edmund. It wasn't premeditated, but it was murder."

"Do you believe him?"

"Well, I don't know. People have murdered for less than a tenure job. But you're right. It does seem very un-Charles-like. But why would an innocent man confess to murder?"

Betsy, who had been busy knitting tiny yellow booties for the upcoming seventeenth grandchild tilted her head to one side in thought. "Well," she mused, "on the T.V. shows, when the innocent person confesses, they are generally protecting someone they love. But that would mean Mildred killed Edmund. And that seems even less likely. Or Charles was protecting a child, but Charles and Mildred never had any children."

C.J. stared at Betsy.

"What?" asked Betsy, beginning to feel somewhat uncomfortable. She did not know what she had said to startle her friend.

"I'll tell you what. You're a complete genius. Poor Charles. What a fool."

"So...he is the killer?" Betsy asked, not completely following.

"No. I don't think so." C.J. sat looking thoughtful. She sipped her coffee, wondering if a single human in the history of the planet Earth had ever behaved rationally. Certainly no one in the economics department at Eaton University ever had.

*****

It was after eight p.m. on Friday night, and C.J. Whitmore was still at work. Between the extra classes she was teaching and the needy people wandering into her office "needing to talk," C.J. was behind on her research agenda. Ever the professional, she was staying back late to ensure she met the deadlines of her upcoming conferences and journal revisions. Walter emailed, asking if they could "catch up for a cup of coffee." C.J. just pressed delete. She wasn't in the mood to deal with that issue.

Tired, but wanting to put in a few more hours at her desk, C.J. wandered down to the Smythe Lounge. The coffee was stale, burnt and distinctly unappetizing. Faced with the choice of walking down the street to get a well-made latte or making mediocre coffee herself, C.J. decided to brew another pot. It was the option with the least people contact.

While she was listening to the gurgles and gargles of Mr. Coffee, Annika Jonsdottir came into the room.

"Hello Annika," said C.J., laughing to herself. She was clearly a people-magnet today. Actually, C.J. wasn't surprised to see the girl here so late. Annika was one of the elite, hard-working graduate students.

"Professor Whitmore," Annika bowed her head and stood a respectful distance, waiting for coffee.

C.J. looked over at Annika. What had Betsy said? There was something wrong with the girl? The girl was stressed. That was it. Looking at her, C.J. could see she looked a little tired and....flighty? Now that C.J.

thought about it, she realized Annika looked like a rabbit that would jump at the slightest sound.

C.J. went back to making coffee and made two cups. "White or black?" she asked Annika.

"Oh. Me? Just black. Thanks."

C.J. doubted that was true, but figured the girl was asking for the coffee of least trouble. Well, she couldn't help that. She handed Annika her coffee and suggested they sit down.

Annika froze.

"You know, I don't bite after dark. You'll be quite safe," C.J. assured, laughing.

Annika smiled and followed her professor over to the blue couches.

"So," C.J. said, "I do heart to hearts like a bull does ballet. Something's troubling you. What's up?"

Annika stared silently at the black depths of her Styrofoam coffee cup.

"Is it a boy?"

"No. No," Annika paused. She clearly had something to say, and C.J. waited her out. "It's a man."

Mmmm, this is interesting, thought C.J. *Professors and their pickled peckers.*

"Oh, yes?" said C.J., feigning indifference. "A man? Any man in particular?"

"Yes," said Annika unhappily. "Professor Scovill."

Caught by surprise, C.J. snorted coffee out her nose. Walter? Somehow, C.J. had not thought Annika was Walter's type. Too...mature. "Sorry," C.J. said, "I seemed to have swallowed my coffee the wrong way. Professor Scovill, you said?"

"Yes," said Annika. "But not how you are thinking. He is not troubling me in a...intimate...way."

"Oh, good," C.J. sighed in partial relief. "So, what is the trouble?"

"I have a trouble of conscience."

C.J. raised an eyebrow.

"On the day Professor DeBeyer was killed, I was sitting here in the Smythe Lounge at lunchtime. I was sitting over there," Annika pointed to a secluded seat in the back corner, "waiting for Jose. He was supposed to meet me at one-thirty, but he never showed." The girl sighed, sad at the memory of waiting for the boy who did not show.

"At about one-fifteen, I am not exactly sure of the time, Professor Scovill comes into the Smythe Lounge from the 42 Knollwood side and goes across to the 40 Knollwood side. He returns about ten minutes later, or maybe fifteen minutes, I am not too sure as I did not think it was so important at the time."

"I see," said C.J., and she did see.

"I was in the Smythe Lounge for another ten minutes, maybe, until about one-forty. But I didn't see him again. But I overhear you say in Wallaby's that he says he was in his office the whole hour from one until two," said Annika forlornly. "So I do not know what to do. He is a professor. I am a graduate student. I do not want to make trouble."

C.J. patted the young woman on the arm, as you would a horse on the back of the neck. "You did the right thing. I will take care of it from here."

SATURDAY

Walter was thinking of apologizing, and it was actually causing him physical pain. His right eye was twitching, and he was developing a rather itchy rash under his left arm pit. It did not even help that he had spent some "quality time" that morning with an undergraduate possessing perfect skin and an ass like a baby's. Walter was just not the apologizing type.

However, he had calculated the costs and benefits of saying sorry to Jefferson Daniels for his temper tantrum yesterday and decided it was worth the effort. At least, the effort of feigning being sorry.

His outburst of yesterday had been too public. Clearly. As Walter had been forced to answer inane police questions because of it. More to the point, he had wasted a lot of time yesterday answering these questions, as it turned out that Charles had confessed to the crime.

"When you said you crushed Professor DeBeyer like a bug, what did you mean?"

Walter had tried not to sneer at the young policeman when he asked this question. If he was guilty, he wasn't about to say, "Oh yeah. What I meant was I strangled the bastard with his Harvard hoodie." So they were going to get the same answer either way. "I meant it figuratively. That I used my power as Chair of the department to play friendly tit-for-tat games with Professor DeBeyer, such as asking him to teach Econ 101. Obviously I regret my temper outburst. I think we are all feeling stressed by the loss of our dear colleague."

"It sounded like you made a threat on the life of Professor Daniels."

Again Walter wondered if such questioning ever caught a criminal. "Oh yes. That's right. I am planning to kill Jefferson Tuesday at eight. You might want to put that in your calendar."

Of course no one would admit that.

"My goodness! No! Professor Daniels is a very dear friend. I have known him both as a student and colleague. Heavens, I have no plans to kill anyone. As I said, I was just worked up over Edmund's death."

"It sounded like Professor Daniels's comment about paying him forty acres and a mule sparked your loss of temper. Are you in financial distress, Professor Scovill?"

Walter laughed inwardly. That is what these clowns concluded it was all about…financial distress. Well, thank God. "No. I am a very fortunate man. I experience no 'financial distress.'"

Walter walked into the faculty lounge at just before eleven in the morning on Saturday, trying to look repentant and not show his annoyance at having wasted hours with the police the day before. The net effect was closer to constipation than contrition.

Even though it was the weekend, Walter knew he would find people there. Whether it was because the faculty loved their jobs too much or their wives didn't love them enough wasn't always clear. Jefferson was drinking a smoothie and talking with Peter. It was still early and no one else was there yet. Both men looked up when Walter entered the room. An awkward silence fell over the room. Walter cleared his throat. "Yes. Well. I hope no one took what I said yesterday seriously. Just het up over something unrelated to the department."

Ever gracious, Jefferson smiled. "I can't even remember what you said yesterday, Walter. Why don't you join us? We were just discussing the news that Charles admitted to killing Edmund. Is this true?"

Walter nodded. "Yes. It is. Doesn't seem quite right, somehow. Young Stephen. Now he seemed to have the temper. Those Orientals. You can never tell. I would have thought C.J. had it in her, at the right time of the month. But Charles? I wouldn't have guessed he even had the strength. He's gotten so frail over the last year."

Jefferson looked sad. "I know. I know. But if Charles says he did it, and the police find the evidence to support it...I think there are cases where elderly people with dementia can do extraordinary, sometimes violent, things."

Peter nodded. "I've heard something about that too. It is so sad to think of Charles ending his career this way. What will Mildred do?"

"We, meaning the department, will have to make sure she is taken care of," said Jefferson gravely. "It is only right. She is part of the economics family."

Walter listened to this last comment with alarm. What was Jefferson thinking? As Chair, he didn't want to make any sort of financial commitment to the old woman. God himself didn't know how long she would live. But give her an annuity and she sure as hell would never die. The department would be celebrating Mildred's 100th birthday in the Smythe Lounge before you could say "budget deficit." Maybe a one-time grant of $1000. Maybe.

Walter realized that Jefferson was still talking to him. "What?" he asked, ungraciously. Clearly the need to humble himself had passed.

"I said, who is covering his economic history class for the rest of semester?"

"God damn," Walter said, summarizing the situation succinctly for everyone. Obviously, that small detail had not been taken care of. "Um, does anyone else on the faculty know any economic history? It's such a load of crap."

"I hate to suggest it," said Peter rubbing a hand over his head distractedly. "It wouldn't be fair."

"Suggest it," ordered Walter.

"Well, she doesn't do anything with it these days, but I was on the hiring committee for C.J. Whitmore …" Peter faltered out. While he hated to drop C.J. in it, one must put self-preservation ahead of kindness. His work was done. He could guarantee he wasn't teaching that dreadful history course.

Jefferson looked at him. "Peter, are you telling us that C.J., the numbers queen, has a second field area in economic history?"

"Well, yes. Actually, she published a few articles in the area in grad school. But it really isn't fair. She's already teaching an overload by taking Edmund's class and I believe she's now taking on Edmund's Memorial Foundation Committee work."

Walter's eyes sparkled. This was the best news he had heard all morning. Oh. He was going to enjoy telling that pink-booted cow girl that she was now teaching economic history as well. She was going to have that application into UT Austin before the end of the day.

*****

Thank God it is the weekend, thought C.J.

C.J. loved the weekend as she could work uninterrupted by students and teaching. She also indulged herself with a few hours away from the department, such as now. C.J. was almost giddy with delight as she locked her office door behind her in the late morning and headed out to East Elm Park for a hike. The wooded, hilly park, just to the east of the campus, was beginning to turn a splash of red, yellow and orange with the start of fall. With all that was going on, C.J. was eager to scuff her way through the leaves along the hiking trails and clear her thoughts.

As C.J. hurried down the steps of 42 Knollwood, she bumped right into Jose, who was making his way into the building. "Oh. I am so sorry, Jose," C.J. apologized, as she steadied herself against the young graduate student. "You'd think I'd use the eyes God gave me."

Jose murmured that he was fine, and, trying not to look at Professor Whitmore, he started to make his way into the building.

But C.J. was too strong a force. "Wait one moment, will ya?" C.J. requested. "Come walk with me. Don't you just love this time of year, Jose? There was a chill in the air when I got up this morning. The sky is a brilliant blue today, without the haze of summer. The leaves are starting to turn. I swear on my horse's bridle I smell cinnamon everywhere I go."

With the skill of a horsewoman turning a reluctant colt, C.J. maneuvered Jose down the steps and onto Knollwood Place. The young graduate student had managed to evade C.J. yesterday. But he could only escape her for so long. "You know I used to live on a ranch, don't you, Jose?" asked C.J.

Jose nodded silently, but inwardly he was writhing in agony. He was sure that Professor Whitmore was going to lecture him about the incident with Professor Scovill. Perhaps even kick him out of the program.

"Yep. It was a great ranch. Out in Texas. We had all sorts of animals. Cattle of course. Horses. Ducks. Geese. Chickens. A goat. I liked her. Her name was Gertrude."

Jose nodded again, feeling a faint glimmer of hope. "That sounds wonderful. You must miss it."

"Sure do. Not the smell. It sure don't smell like cinnamon on a ranch. But the rest of it I miss.

"Anyway, for awhile, we had a real mean, ole dog. Named him Tex, 'cause he thought he was as important as the whole damn state. And Tex controlled all the other dogs. Wouldn't let them eat unless they did stuff for him. Like, ladies had to…you know…if he wanted it, before they got a meal. And all the other dogs had to bring bones and raid the hen house for Tex. It was something."

"What happened to Tex?"

"We shot that bastard of a dog. Right between the eyes." C.J. kept walking, not looking over at Jose.

"Professor Whitmore," asked Jose, trying to poke holes in her story, "how'd you know what Tex was up to? I don't think the other dogs came and told you."

C.J. smiled, despite herself. Jose Grimaldo was a smart young man. "Actually, Jose," C.J. said in a conspiratorial whisper, as she turned and faced the young graduate student, "one of the dogs sent me an anonymous email in the middle of the night. Knocked me for a loop. Didn't realize the little fellow had his own laptop."

*****

It was lunchtime, and Walter was licking the last of his pastrami-on-rye off his fingers as he hovered over his computer keyboard in anticipation. He couldn't stop smiling. Oh, he was going to enjoy writing this email to C.J. Whitmore.

FROM: Walter Scovill
TO: C.J. Whitmore
SUBJECT: Yep! I am screwing you.

C.J.

It's your lucky day! As of right now, you will now be teaching...

Walter stopped typing. Perhaps a touch too nasty and a little...tyrannical. Maybe, he should start by saying something nice.

FROM: Walter Scovill
TO: C.J. Whitmore
SUBJECT: Great news! Another teaching
assignment!

C.J.

Thanks for pitching in and teaching Edmund's class. Now teach Charles's class.

Walter

Walter reread the email. Again, the ending was too abrupt. What did he really want to say? *You, my little Texas rose, are the thorn that is causing a pestilent and gangrenous wound in my otherwise happy existence. I hate having you in the department, and I am trying to make your life so miserable that you will resign. So here is yet another odious task for you.* Walter sighed. Emails could come back and haunt you like ghosts of dead lovers. He couldn't put that in writing.

FROM: Walter Scovill
TO: C.J. Whitmore
SUBJECT: Econ history course

C.J.

Thanks for being such a great faculty member. I appreciate your teaching Edmund's class and serving on the Edmund DeBeyer Memorial Foundation Committee. Your commitment to the department in these trying times has not gone unnoticed.

With Charles out of action, we all have to do our bit, and I must turn to you again. Economic history is such a narrow specialty, and you are the only other faculty member with the knowledge and skills to teach his course. For the remainder of the semester, I will need you to teach his economic history class, which is on Tuesday and Thursdays, 10:40 - 11:50. Please let me know what teaching assistants you need to make this task easier.

Walter

Walter reread the email once more. Much better. That was an email that the Dean could read, and Walter would look both civil and conciliatory. Offering teaching assistants? What more could the woman want?

With an evil grin, he pressed send.

*****

Mary Beth had met a group of girlfriends at Bindi's for a late brunch to tell them all about "Life in the Shadow of a Murderer." There is no point in being almost murdered if you can't be the center of attention.

But even Mary Beth had to admit, there is good attention and bad attention. Unlike today, yesterday was bad attention. She had to talk to the police. Again. Telling your story to the police is only cool, like, the first time. Not the fourth and fifth and sixth retellings. As Mary Beth told the policeman yesterday, "No offence, but I'd prefer to get a Brazilian than sit here and talk with you. Are we, like, almost done?"

And then it turned out that Professor Covington was the killer, not Professor Choi. Which made no sense at all. That's like your sweet old grandpa suddenly becoming an axe murderer. But, whatever.

And if it wasn't bad enough that she had been working with not one but two murderers, Mary Beth was quite peeved that Jefferson Daniels had not been his flirty self yesterday.

"What am I, a big hair dye job from Trenton?" she vented angrily to her friends. It did not occur to Mary Beth that Jefferson could be upset or distracted because of his colleague's confession, or the death of his friend.

Well, maybe I should just do something about that, thought Mary Beth impulsively as she left Bindi's, with a confidence that should probably be attributed to the three pitchers of sangrias that Mary Beth and her friends had consumed over brunch. So, after popping a tic tac and checking that she was attired in appropriately skimpy underclothing, Mary Beth ventured into the department on a Saturday and knocked on Jefferson Daniels's door.

No answer.

Mary Beth knocked again, this time a little louder. Still no answer.

Mary Beth tried the door handle to see if the door was locked. If it wasn't, she would write him a cute note and hope for a better day on Monday. The handle turned, and she cautiously opened the door, calling out as she did, "Yoo hoo. Professor Daniels. It's me. Mary Beth."

There was still no answer, so Mary Beth entered Jefferson's office. She walked over to the desk and started to search for a blank piece of paper when something caught her eye. Was that Professor Daniels's sneaker sticking out from the left side of the desk?

*****

At 42 Knollwood, any calming effects of C.J.'s hike had evaporated. She was currently composing a reply to

Walter's email. She had wanted to write something along the lines of

FROM: C.J. Whitmore
TO: Walter Scovill
SUBJECT: RE: Econ history course

Walter,

Go screw yourself!

C.J.

Or

FROM: C.J. Whitmore
TO: Walter Scovill
SUBJECT: RE: Econ history course

Walter,

If I have to teach Economic History, then I will make sure you are history.

C.J.

Or

FROM: C.J. Whitmore
TO: Walter Scovill
SUBJECT: RE: Econ history course

Walter,

Sure, I would love to teach another course. But, of course, I would need the students to lick my shoes clean first. Could you take care of that?

Thanks!

C.J.

However, C.J. refrained. As her daddy would say, any mule can deliver a kick. But only the finest racehorses keep their heads down and last the distance. She was just starting to work on a somewhat more civil reply when she heard Mary Beth screaming.

C.J. paused. It sounded like Mary Beth was yelling, "He's dead! He's dead!"

SUNDAY

It was nine in the morning, and Walter sat stiffly in an uncomfortable leather chair that he suspected had great historical importance. Probably belonged to Eli Whitney's grandfather, if Walter had to guess by the lack of padding supporting his butt. Walter grimaced a smile at the three men who sat in front of him. He was feeling far too cranky about Jefferson dying to experience any sense of submissiveness. "So, here we are again," he joked.

No one laughed.

This is going to be a long day, thought Walter, wearily. *Murder is such a time-suck.*

"Professor   Scovill."   The   President   of   Eaton University   announced   Walter's   name   like   an   irate headmaster calling a recalcitrant child into the office. "I am missing my tee time at the Elm Grove Country Club. Clearly, I am not happy."

Walter noticed he had been demoted from Walt to Professor Scovill. Never a good sign if one is hoping for promotion.

"Under   your   tenure   as   Chair   of   the   economics department,   two,   I   repeat   TWO,"   the   President   was beginning   to   get   worked   up   and   had   turned   a disconcerting   shade   of   puce,   "potential   Nobel   prize winners have been killed. First one was strangled. And yesterday afternoon, the second one was found by a secretary dead on his office floor. Cause of death is still to be determined. Those Nobel Prizes are lost to us forever. Forever!"

Hmmm, thought Walter, unimpressed that his own Sunday had been disrupted to listen to this tirade, *not my problem*.

"As I am sure you know," continued the President, without apparently stopping for breath, "a person can only be awarded the Nobel Prize if they are alive. A key quality that your faculty seems to be lacking these days. Perhaps, Professor Scovill, you didn't realize that Harvard was already up by one in the Nobel Prize race. I know, as Harvard's President is merciless in reminding me of the fact every time we meet."

The President paused for air and glared at Walter. Walter stared back with unblinking eyes.

The Dean of Arts and Sciences and the Provost, who were also in the room, studied their Italian loafer shoes with intense interest. They did not want the President to shift his rage their direction. It was best he believed that Walter Scovill was solely responsible for letting a murderer run rampant through the economics department. After all, what was Walter doing with his time? Surely, as Chair, he was supposed to keep the faculty in line.

Walter had not slept well since C.J. had walked in on the shoe polishing scene in his office. He was tired. He was frustrated. And now, just because Jefferson Daniels, an overrated faculty member in Walter's opinion, had been murdered, through no fault of Walter's, he was being treated like the whipping boy of an arrogant old man. Walter did not see any irony in this situation. Instead, feeling the uncontrollable anger of a powerful person made powerless, Walter met the President's angry gaze defiantly.

"Are you honestly asking me why I didn't foresee the murder of two of my faculty? Why I am not omnipresent and all knowing?" Walter's voice was getting louder, and he was gradually rising from his chair to match it. The Dean and the Provost were looking up now. The meeting had taken a distinct turn. "I'll tell you why I couldn't see what was going on. Because my head spends most of the day buried deep in your butt, and it's damn dark up there!"

With the three administrators staring at him open-mouthed, Walter turned and left with a resounding slam of the heavy oak door.

*****

Mary Beth was standing on the steps of 40 Knollwood, dressed in her "person who discovered the body" outfit. After careful consultation with her friends, Mary Beth decided against all black. She needed to distinguish herself from the mourners. Vulture-like reporters, scavenging for someone with first-hand details, were confronted with a young woman in a tight black mini-skirt, a fitted red top with plunging neckline and more footage than they planned of a black, lace, push-up bra. Mary Beth completed the ensemble with five inches of heels and a manicure that spelled out DEATH on each hand.

"I was sitting at brunch with my BFFs, eating my French Toast, and a shiver ran up my spine," Mary Beth explained, her false eyelashes wide with imagined fright. "It was like a ghost was walking over my grave. Somehow, I knew that something was wrong with our dearest Professor Daniels."

"Excuse me, Miss Sanders, are you saying you knew it was Professor Daniels who had died before you even found the body?"

"Well," Mary Beth hesitated, torn between the truth and a really good story, "I had a really, really strong feeling. It was like Professor Daniels was trying to, like …let me know. And I was right. Because when I went by the department after brunch..." Here, Mary Beth stopped and delicately dabbed at her eyes.

Another reporter raised her hand. "Why did you finish brunch when you thought Professor Daniels was in danger? Why not just go and make sure he was okay?"

Mary Beth looked confused for a moment. "Oh, well, I didn't want to look silly if I was, like, wrong. But," Mary Beth hung her head, paused dramatically, and tried to look desperately sad, "but I wasn't wrong. Someone had taken dear Professor Daniels from us."

The questions continued, Mary Beth kept making up answers, and the reporters kept writing them down. The death of one professor was a story that had come and gone. The death of two...a serial killer on the loose in the economics department at Eaton University. That was not worth inches in the paper, but yards.

*****

Of course, the unintended victim of the second murder was Charles. He found himself released from Elm Grove City Jail at ten o'clock that morning, despite his protestations of guilt. "I killed the man. Why don't you believe me? It was me, I tell you, me!"

The uniformed officer who was walking with Charles looked at him sadly. Old age, what a bitch. This one was clearly a loony. Must be that Old Timer's disease. The one that causes you to lose your mind. There was no way it was this dude. He was safely locked up when the second murder occurred. His story just didn't check out. Crazy...that's what you had to be to confess to a murder you didn't do. Crazy.

*****

FROM: C.J. Whitmore
TO: Walter Scovill
SUBJECT: RE: Econ history course

Walter,

Thank you for acknowledging my work in supporting the department. It is so nice to have one's efforts recognized. Until your email, I had been considering the position at UT Austin, but after your kind words, I simply couldn't leave Eaton University. You have made me feel part of the Eaton family.

Of course, I would have been very willing to pitch in and teach Charles's class. However, now that Charles has been released, thankfully, there will be no need.

Of course, we are now faced with the sad task of finding a teacher for Jefferson's class. Sadly, I am unable to assist, as it occurs at the same time as Edmund's class. But I believe you have that time slot free and are so knowledgeable in the subject Jefferson was teaching. As you say, we all have to do our bit.

C.J.

Mildred had called C.J. early in the morning with the good news that Charles was coming home that day, and C.J., thankful that she hadn't had time to reply to Walter's email yesterday, had been perfecting her response ever since. Just as C.J. pressed send and was getting ready to meet Betsy for a rare Sunday coffee (Betsy was letting her detective work a.k.a curiosity impact her weekends now), there was a knock at her office door. C.J. checked her watch. Just before eleven. Damn. She would be late. "Come in," she called out.

A tired, unsmiling detective walked in. "Professor Whitmore?" he asked.

"The one and only," said C.J. "Take a load off." C.J. indicated the chairs opposite her desk. "You are here about dear Jeffie, I am guessing."

"Yes, Ma'am. I do have a few questions."

C.J. nodded her head. "I think we all do. How did Jeffie die?"

The policeman sized her up. "He was poisoned. It looks like cyanide poisoning."

"Poisoned? Like a rat? Any chance it was suicide?"

The policeman raised an eyebrow. "Now that's an interesting question. Was Professor Daniels a depressed person?"

"No. Not at all. He had too much energy. The man ran miles every day and flirted more than he should have. But he was very sad about Professor DeBeyer's death. I wouldn't have thought he would have...but I just wondered..." C.J. petered out and fidgeted nervously.

"Ma'am, am I right in thinking you wondered if he might have committed suicide because he felt so guilty for killing Professor DeBeyer?"

C.J. looked pained. "No. Maybe. Well, yes. The thought did cross my mind."

"Well, rest easy, if that is the right thing to say. It was not suicide. Professor Daniels was murdered. Cyanide was found in his protein powder. If he was going to commit suicide, he would have just stirred it into his drink. The poison was deliberately placed there, a deadly powdery weapon."

"Oh my God! Where do you buy cyanide?"

"Well, frankly, you can buy anything on the web these days. But, you don't have to buy cyanide. If you are smart enough, you can make it from almonds."

"So, there is someone out there who has killed two of the professors in this department?"

"It looks that way. So, what did you see yesterday afternoon?"

C.J. tried very hard to remember. "Well, I was in my office working from about one, after I got back from my hike. As you realize, my office is not in the same building as Jefferson's. But Jeffie dropped by my office shortly after one. He had been convinced that Walter killed Edmund ever since Walter lost his temper in the faculty lounge. Jeffie wanted to tell me that Walter tried to make nice that morning, but he didn't believe a word of it. Jeffie was ranting that he was going to ensure Walter went down for the murder of Edmund. He didn't care that Charles had confessed. He thought that Charles was just losing it because he was so old."

The detective nodded and made some notes. "What did you say?"

"I told Jeffie to go for a run and clear his head, which is what he did. Well, he said he was going to. I didn't actually see him running. But he was in running clothes when I saw him…you know."

"Yes. I am sorry you had to see that. Was there anything else that happened that afternoon?"

"Not that I can think of. The department was quiet because it was the weekend. Most people were at home or working with their doors closed. But then at about three-ish, Mary Beth started screaming. I could hear her in my office, and that's one building over. So I ran across and saw Jeffie lying on the floor behind his desk, dead."

"That's very clear. Now, Professor Whitmore…" the detective cleared his throat uncomfortably.

C.J. looked at him with interest. What was it he didn't want to say? She waited him out.

"Do you have any thoughts on why a young secretary was in the office of Professor Daniels on a Saturday?"

C.J. let out a snort of laughter, causing the detective to raise his eyebrows. "Mary Beth was in search of a bank balance to marry, if you get what I mean. She had fastened her talons into Jeffie, and he didn't help matters as he was born a-flirtin'."

The detective nodded. An old plot line.

"I am guessing she came in yesterday to bat her eyelash extensions at Jeffie, in hopes of scoring a Saturday night dinner date."

The detective nodded again. "One other question," he asked. "It has struck me as somewhat strange, but am I right in thinking Mary Beth is the only administrative assistant for the entire economics department? Surely, there should be more for a department this size."

C.J. smiled wryly. "Oh, there are more, but you just can't find 'em. It's so awful working around Walter and his merry men that, over the years, they've migrated to the Business School building or even across to the math department. They always have a water tight excuse… usually citing some OSHA code that is being broken. The University lets it happen as it's better than some sexual harassment lawsuit. It's not so bad now that most work is done via email. Mary Beth sticks it out because she, of course, is trying to land one of the econ profs as a husband."

The detective tried to look unfazed by this explanation of complete dysfunction, but his face said, *"Why have only two of you people been murdered so far?"*

"Well," he said with false cheer, "I appreciate your time."

As the detective rose to go, C.J. stopped him. "I have one question."

"Yes?" The detective looked at her, uncertain if he was going to humor her curiosity.

"Was the cyanide found in a container of protein powder that was full or partly empty?"

"It was quite full. Why do you want to know?"

"I'm not sure. I guess more data is always better than less. Thanks."

*****

Walter was wondering if the President would revoke his tenure due to issues of professionalism. Almost two hours had passed and still no word. Perhaps he was going to get away with his little temper tantrum. Walter admonished himself. It was an amateur mistake to allow himself to be bothered by administrators.

Some policemen would be "stopping by" in a few minutes. Walter knew they would want to talk about the fight he had with Jefferson. He could anticipate the conversation.

"It seems you didn't like either of the dead men."

Well, that was true enough. But then, Walter didn't really like anyone but himself.

"You were heard threatening the life of Professor Daniels."

Yeah well, sticks and stones and all that.

"Where were you yesterday?"

Killing Professor Daniels. Not.

In my office, just like now, of course. Walter looked under the desk and smiled. "Tutoring an undergraduate." Just like now.

There was a sharp knock at the door.

"Come in," called out Walter, who waved in the two policemen with more graciousness than they were expecting.

"Please, take a seat," said Walter expansively. "I'm in no hurry."

*****

Betsy was waiting in Wallaby's coffee shop. She knew that C.J. might be late, if she showed at all. The economics department was a hive of police officers and reporters. As the second person on the scene, and the first person of any notable intelligence, there were many questions only C.J. could answer.

Betsy sipped her double mocha and pulled out her crochet work. She was willing to wait.

"Betsy?" a voice asked, questioningly.

Betsy looked up.

"Professor Covington," Betsy cried, "well, it is really wonderful to see you. Please, take a seat."

Charles, turning his hearing aids on as he eased himself into a seat, grunting as he sat down. "It's always good to sit down," he explained to Betsy. "The legs aren't what they used to be."

Betsy laughed. "You don't have to explain that to me. Between the arthritic right knee, the plantar fasciitis in the left foot, the achy left hip and the bunions, it is a wonder I am ambulatory."

"When did this happen?" asked Charles, somewhat absently. "I still feel like a young man, my body just isn't keeping pace."

Betsy patted Charles on the knee. "Don't worry yourself over it. If you feel young, then that's all that matters. Now, why aren't you at home with your beautiful wife today?"

Charles grimaced. "It's the Sunday Quilting Bee. The ladies of the church gather after the service to stitch blanket things for the homeless. And, trust me, nothing would stop that. Not even my release from incarceration. I stopped home briefly this morning to shower and change, but thought it best if I step out of the house for awhile, so they could gossip about me and my little stay in jail in peace."

Betsy nodded understandingly. That was the thoughtfulness of a man who had been married a long, long time. "Charles, you have known me since I was a fresh-faced graduate student. Since you've brought it up, what were you thinking, confessing to a murder?"

Charles looked down at the table in front of him. "Well, now, that's mighty complicated."

"What's so complicated? I can't believe you killed the man."

Charles looked sheepish. "Well, maybe I didn't. But," he added with a lot more passion, "they were all asking so many questions."

"Who? Who was asking questions?"

"The police. And people in the department. They were asking Mildred, too. I wanted to make all the questions stop. Isn't a man entitled to any privacy these days?"

"Well, of course you are," Betsy assured the obviously stressed Charles, and allowing her commonsense to override her curiosity, Betsy deftly changed the topic and began to talk about her grandchildren.

*****

In an unprecedented move, on the Sunday afternoon following Jefferson's death, the economics department gathered for a faculty meeting. Faculty meetings did not occur on weekend days. But, the death of a second colleague made for exceptional times.

Walter, as Chair of the department, had called the meeting. It was apparent by the outrageous number of emails in his inbox that there was a high level of interest among the faculty as to what was going on. An interest that Walter did not have the time nor desire to deal with on a one-on-one level. If Walter had bothered to read any of these emails, he would have also known there was a high level of irritation amongst the ranks with the intrusive questioning from the police and the media. Of note, it was not clear that there was an overwhelming sense of grief, but at least one or two junior faculty had shown the courtesy of expressing words of condolence.

Well, for people who wanted some answers, they sure are taking their time in arriving, thought Walter sourly, noting that it was well after the planned start time of two o'clock and less than a quarter of the expected faculty was present. What's more, those who were present were junior faculty and so of little consequence.

Peter came rushing in at ten after two with an insincere and hurried, "Sorry I'm late," and promptly opened his laptop and started taking care of his daily influx of emails.

Walter was surprised to see Charles arrive next, resplendent in his red suspenders and green polka dot bow tie. Surely the old boy would want to take some time off. Maybe consult with a doctor, preferably a psychiatrist. "Charles," Walter greeted his colleague without much enthusiasm, "not confessing to any crimes today I see. Well, don't just stand there. Take a seat. This meeting was supposed to start fifteen minutes ago."

Charles walked slowly and a little unsteadily towards the front. His teetering was due partly to his aging legs and partly to the three gin and tonics he had drunk just prior to his arrival. Anything to make spending time with Walter bearable.

Just as Charles was easing himself into his seat, the room fell silent and seemed to take a collective inhale. C.J. had walked in with Stephen Choi by her side. C.J. glanced around the room with a smile and broke the silence. "My goodness. It's quieter in here than a graveyard in winter. Were you all just talking about me? 'Cause if so, I hope it was something nice. My birthday is coming up, and I would just love one of those bull riding belt buckles, if y'all are stuck for a gift."

C.J. strode confidently toward the front half of the room, dragging Stephen with her and leaving open-mouthed colleagues in her wake. "Honey," she whispered to him, "if they think you are a murderer, where you place your patootie isn't going to change that fact. Might as well take the A-reserve seating."

Stephen, who had flown back into town on a red-eye, after his girlfriend had discovered she really only wanted to be "just friends" now that Stephen wasn't going to be an Eaton University professor, just sighed. He wasn't strong enough to take the politics of academia today, and he told C.J. as much.

C.J. just laughed. "What is that great quote by Kissinger? Something about the reason university politics are so vicious is because the stakes are so small. Stephen, sweetie, nothing we do here really matters, but we make each other miserable doing it. That's the definition of a 'dot edu.' If you want kumbaya, you want a 'dot org'."

Stephen stared at C.J. "Do you really believe that?"

"Of course. I'm just here for my own mental pleasuring. And because I like to have the summers off. If I really wanted to change the world, I would get a real job."

"Do you think that's why Jefferson was resigning?"

C.J. looked at Stephen with a start. She had completely forgotten that Jefferson was resigning. With all the fuss over the murders and Charles confessing, it had slipped her mind that Jefferson had decided academia wasn't for him. What was he going to do again? Oh. That's right. Be an alpaca farmer. In Colorado. No. Not Colorado. Close to Colorado, but more exotic. New Mexico? Could that be right? Please. Someone as urban as Jeffie wouldn't have lasted a week ranching in New Mexico.

Stephen interrupted her musings. "C.J.? Are you alright? You look completely lost in thought."

C.J. refocused on Stephen with a start. "Sorry. I had just forgotten that Jeffie was planning to live his dream.

What a darn shame he wasn't able to. The whole thing is just too darn sad for words."

Stephen looked like he wanted to console C.J., but was unsure of the appropriate words. Before he could stumble through some awkward, but well-meant phrases, Walter interrupted. "Thank you for coming, even if you have once again shown an astonishing inability to tell time. The only agenda item for today's meeting is the death of Professor Jefferson Daniels. I have received your many, many emails. I realize you want details. I will share the few I have."

Murmurs rippled around the room like waves washing ashore, ebbing in and out. This did not sound satisfactory. C.J., not expecting to hear anything she didn't already know, opened her laptop and began to check her email. Time was, after all, a scarce resource. Charles, sitting in the front row, had his hearing aids turned up high. Meetings about murder were worth his attention. Peter had stopped checking his email and closed his laptop about half-way. A sign of interest but he wasn't fully committing to Walter. Stephen sat, eyes downcast, fiddling with his ball point pen. He had timed his return terribly. Did people realize that he had come back into town after Jefferson had died? He would have to make sure they knew somehow.

Walter looked down at his notes. "This is what I have learned from the police. You may have read some of this in the paper already. Professor Jefferson Daniels was murdered. Cyanide was added to his protein powder, which he consumed after his run yesterday. This method is in contrast to Professor DeBeyer, who was strangled. However, I think it is safe to assume they were killed by the same person."

Here Walter was interrupted by a junior professor sitting towards the back. "So, are we all going to be systematically picked off, one-by-one, until no economics faculty remain at Eaton University? Is that the idea? The murderer hates Eaton University economists?"

"The motive is not transparently clear. But as Edmund and Jefferson did the same research and that research received a lot of public attention, including from the Nobel committee, then I think a safe assumption is that the motive relates to their work."

Another faculty, an intense young environmental economist, raised a hand. "So you are guaranteeing our safety? No one else is going to be killed?"

Walter looked over his glasses and glared at the young economist. Where were the intellects of today? The thinkers. The scholars. "Of course I am not guaranteeing your safety. What an absurd concept. You could walk across Knollwood to your office and get hit by a car. I have no control over that. Likewise, the murderer could meet you, be as irritated as I am now, and decide to do the world a favor by killing you. I, also, cannot control that. All I am merely saying is that, given the two victims thus far were pre-eminent economists doing cutting-edge, life-altering research, I think the probability that you, an economist of little value, will be murdered is low."

"That's what I like about you, Walter," said C.J., looking up from her computer. "You are always such a comfort."

Walter, missing the sarcasm, nodded his head in thanks. "Because we would all like to have the killer behind bars," Walter continued, "we must endure the questioning by the police."

Everyone broke into chatter at this. Stories of policemen and women interrupting their days and their precious research time. Tales of intrusive questions, having to tell of "private study sessions" with students.

It was embarrassing and, frankly, unnecessary. They had Ph.D.'s. Their word should be enough.

Walter cleared his throat and brought the room to silence. "You just told me you would like to know who the killer is. So, *ergo*, answer their questions."

Charles spoke up, his speech a little slurred from pre-loading before the meeting. "Oh, it's easy to work out the killer. Follow the money. History shows money leads you to the killer every time. Follow the money, damn it."

Walter cleared his throat again. Edmund had been right. It was time for Charles to retire—past time. Obviously the old man needed psychiatric help. First he confessed to a murder he didn't commit, and now he was ranting about money being the answer to the crimes, which made no sense when Edmund had started a foundation, and...

"Where did Jefferson leave his money?" Charles demanded belligerently.

Walter knew this information, having had a call that morning from Edmund's widow, of all people, explaining Jefferson's will. He wondered briefly if he should keep the facts to himself, but then decided if you shared information with one person, you were sharing it with the world. Unless, of course, the secret was his. "As you might have known, Jefferson didn't have any family. The aunt who had raised him passed away several years ago, and there was no other family to speak of. Jefferson looked up to Edmund, almost like a father. So he left everything in his will to Edmund and his wife. Lisa called me today to see how to transfer the funds to Edmund's foundation, since that is where all of Edmund's money is being invested. She didn't think it was right to profit from Edmund and Jefferson's friendship."

Several faculty stared stiffly ahead, distraught at the thought of all that money being funneled into Edmund's useless foundation. It was heartbreaking, but economists don't cry.

Charles pursed his lips together. He was still trying to puzzle out the mystery.

Walter looked at him. "I am afraid history has let you down. Money isn't the answer. No one benefits. It's all in the foundation."

Throughout all of this, C.J. had been busy deleting emails from her computer. No, she did not want to join the Eaton University Scrapbookers Club. It was very nice of the IT department to tell her they were updating the computer server at three on Sunday morning. But she had tenure now, so she was going to be asleep then. It was a new and very pleasant luxury. It looked like Eaton was going to be playing a football game against some equally untalented team this weekend. C.J. had gone to one game and seen the mascot, the little pug dog named Adorable Don, run onto the field. The poor little mite. Looked so confused. But he was doing better than Don the First, who was stuffed and mounted in a glass case in one of the reception halls on campus. That was just plain creepy. No, thought C.J., she would pass on watching both the substandard football and the undergraduates drink until they threw up. Limited entertainment value there. Oh wait, here was an email from Charlotte, her star undergraduate student. Charlotte, as usual, had a very intelligent question about the class material. Today she was making excellent connections to examples of demand and supply in other markets, such as the markets for slaves.

Walter was still droning on up front. There would be counseling available. C.J. rolled her eyes. Like anyone would go to that. Walter would be accepting ideas for a fitting memorial for the next two weeks. C.J. laughed inwardly. Clearly, Walter had been badgered by the Dean or the Provost or even the President. No more trying to hide the murders under the proverbial rug. Obviously the Eaton Media Machine now wanted to turn this into a PR event to build unity.

C.J. googled the *The Pug Post* to see the latest coverage.

DAILY DOUBLE: TWO MURDERS FOR THE PRICE OF ONE!

What your parents didn't know their tuition dollar would buy. As the economists at Eaton University continue to be picked off, questions should be asked. Is being exposed to this type of violent crime what Eatonians should expect?

I approached the Eaton University President with this question. Is murder now a weekly or daily expectation on the Eaton University campus? Should we expect other violent crime to increase?

The president was not willing to accept that crime was increasing. "The deaths of these two wonderful scholars were isolated incidents, and I hope the perpetrator will be brought to justice soon. In the meantime, I believe this is a time for the Eaton University community to come together to mourn our lost Eatonians, remember their contributions, and move forward as a school."

The article continued, but C.J. stopped reading. Her email alerted her to a new message.

Jose? That was unexpected. C.J. hadn't heard a word from him since yesterday when she had cornered him outside the department. She had begun to think she had been too forward with him. C.J. opened the email, quickly closed it and refocused her attention on Walter.

"Finally," wound up Walter, "it turns out that Jefferson was a member of a church here in Elm Grove. Who knew?" asked Walter in a way that suggested that if Walter did not know, then no one would. "So this means that the funeral will not be at one of the churches on the Square. Rather there will be a memorial service tonight at five o'clock at," Walter paused to look at his notes, "St. Andrews. In case you are unfamiliar with this church, St. Andrews is an Episcopal church. But, it is, um, well, it's on the other side of Main Street."

An uncomfortable silence hung in the air. Everyone knew what Walter was trying to say. This was not an Eaton University church. This was an Elm Grove church, where black people, poor people, and, God forbid, even homeless people would be in attendance. This was a church where women would be moved to cry out "Hallelujah" during the service, and men might mumble, "Praise the Lord." And in such a church, the choirs would sing loudly and in tune and sound as if they really did believe in and love their Christ and Savior.

To the Walters of this world, such a place was very disconcerting and seemed quite uncalled for.

*****

The Episcopal church of St. Andrews was indeed, as Walter so delicately phrased it, on "the other side" of Main Street. It was located in the Elm Grove South neighborhood, an area famous for Jimmy's Pizza (the best pizza in Elm Grove, unless you were a fan of the pepperoni at Sal's Diner), an abundance of cannoli bakeries, and, somewhat out of character, a cherry blossom festival. Elm Grove South was also close to the Amtrak station and, consequently, was a favorite hang out for the homeless, the hungry and the high in Elm Grove.

Although the building of St. Andrews could be considered as beautiful as any church found on the Elm Grove Town Square, with its rising stone spire, stained glass windows and aged wood pews, that is where the similarity ended. St. Andrews prided itself on communicating with God through the fusion of Jazz and Soul. The ten commandments did not say anything about having to sing the Lord's hymns out of tune and in a monotone that would convince the strongest believer that God was yesterday's news. This church rocked, with its congregants clapping, and saxophones wailing. The Lord was indeed lifted up, often with a little impov along the way.

St. Andrews also had the disconcerting habit of opening its doors to everyone. The wealthy and the poor. Black and white. Gay and straight. Housed and homeless. Sober, high, recovering, teetotaler, relapsed and sponsor. All were welcome, indeed encouraged, to think of St. Andrews as home.

St. Andrews tried valiantly to cater to every aspect of community life. The Reverend Tayshon Jackson blessed the pets of the congregation once a month and kept his phobias to himself when the snakes and tarantulas were brought to the steps of the church. *After all*, he thought to himself as he breathed in deeply, *they are God's creatures, too, and the serpent was just a metaphor.* The church held Loaves and Fishes every Saturday, offering food and clothing to those in need. Tayshon had always known he could rely on Jefferson Daniels to take the early morning shift, helping out, offering both food and company. Tayshon had so hoped Jefferson would find a nice girl from the church to marry. He encouraged Jefferson to come to Thursday Vespers, a relaxed evening of Jazz, scriptures, and, often, flirting. The congregants were, after all, human. But while Jefferson was charming to all the ladies, he didn't seek anyone out.

Today St. Andrews was going to provide a place for the community to grieve. Reverend Jackson looked somberly around the church. He knew that the memorial service for Professor Daniels was going to pull a huge crowd. He couldn't actually call it a funeral, as the body wasn't going to be released by the State for quite awhile. But the parishioners wanted to celebrate Jefferson's life now.

Extra seating had already been set up at the back of the church. The ladies of the parish had been stopping by with their best casseroles, home-baked breads, pies, and cakes all day for the celebration of life. The kitchen at the church was overloaded with crockpots, Pyrex and Tupperware. For Brother Daniels, no recipe was too difficult. No cream of mushroom soup, Velveeta cheese or Redi-whip was spared. Another, very select group of women had been arranging flowers. The flower committee was a coveted job and one Reverend Tayshon left to his wife to sort out. He did not understand why everyone couldn't lend a hand in these things. When he said this, his wife just rolled her eyes. Scanning the church, Tayshon had to admit that however it was done, it worked. The sprays of lilies and whatever those little flowers with them were called looked very nice. Very nice indeed.

His flock had been expressing their sorrow and their prayers on the church's Facebook page. Sometimes he wondered if anyone read the damn site. Was he just posting prayers to please God and the Archbishop, who liked to see that the church was keeping up with technology? The Archbishop himself tweeted his prayers (a practice that kept them, thankfully, short.) But when Tayshon had posted the announcement about Jefferson's death, the website had gone into overload with prayers, memories and outreach to other parishioners. Making sure the ones in AA stayed sober. Keeping the ones prone to overdose company. All the things a church should do.

His less computer savvy congregants had been writing their prayers for Jefferson on the two prayer chalkboards that stood outside the church doors. Normally, the prayers ranged from "my sobriety" and "a job" to "peace on earth" and "my family" and, occasionally, "this wonderful church," though Tayshon didn't see the latter very often. He noticed that praying tended to be a self-focused activity. But now, the boards were covered with "For the Prof," "The guy who gave food on Saturdays," "Jefferson, one of our great Jazz singers," "Our brother in Christ," "With the Lord now," "That I may show forgiveness to the person who took Jefferson from us," and "To our brother."

With a sigh, Reverend Jackson went to the front doors of the church and opened them wide. There were already small groups of people milling around on the street, dressed in their finest. It was his time to provide comfort and to show the Lord's healing.

"Come," he said. "Let us celebrate the life of Brother Daniels."

*****

When C.J. and Betsy arrived at the church at four-thirty, the place was already rocking. The contrast to the funeral of Edmund DeBeyer could not help but be noticed. Now, instead of economists and administrators somberly in attendance, it appeared most of Elm Grove's townsfolk were out in force. Men, women and children were standing in the pews singing and clapping, while a jazz band crooned the music up front. An African-American man, who appeared to be the leader of the church, interrupted occasionally, and asked for an "Amen" to celebrate the life of Brother Daniels. As one, the congregation swelled with a joyous and heartfelt "Amen," full of love for Jefferson.

"Oh my," said Betsy, surveying the scene.

"What are you waiting for?" asked C.J., dragging her friend by the hand. "Let's celebrate Jefferson!"

*****

As the person who discovered the body, Mary Beth figured she would have a special role at the funeral. Perhaps the minister would mention her in his speech. Or people would want to take pictures of her next to the casket. Either way, a special outfit was clearly required.

Despite having only hours to prepare, Mary Beth managed eleven conversations with her best friend Annabelle, two shopping trips, and one bloated credit card. She was ready to mourn.

Atop Mary Beth's head was a black pillbox hat with a black netting veil. Sprouting out the top of the hat were three black ostrich feathers, dyed orange around the edges. Her body was encased, like an overstuffed sausage, in a short, skin-tight, black dress with orange panels down the sides. Unfortunately, also like a sausage, little bits of Mary Beth were bursting out at the seams. Mary Beth teetered on five-inch, orange, leopard-print pumps and she had carefully selected a manicure of black nails with orange tear drops. The outfit was completed with a bright orange, feather boa. Mary Beth was extremely pleased with the ensemble—distinctive, sexy, and clearly grieving. To the rest of the world, the decision of black with orange accent colors, and the choice of clothes themselves, regrettably lent the outfit a Halloweenish feel.

Mary Beth arrived at the church at just before five o'clock. The perfect time to be photographed ascending the steps into the church. But, owing to a 22 car pile-up in a flash fog on I-95 that afternoon and a hurricane taking an unexpected turn towards the east coast, there was not a photographer or reporter in sight. The only people who cared about the life and death of Jefferson Daniels were already inside the church.

Mary Beth hung around outside for another ten minutes, but then gave up and went inside. The church was full of people! And not Eaton University people.

Like, people people. And they were singing and stomping their feet and playing the saxophone. This was not like the funeral for Professor DeBeyer. Mary Beth spotted one woman who was sitting quietly and who looked sort of familiar. She went over and sat next to her.

"Hi! I'm Mary Beth. I discovered the body," Mary Beth introduced herself.

The woman, who already looked quite pale, went a ghostly shade of white. "Oh. How...ghastly. I'm Lisa DeBeyer."

"Oh right! Professor DeBeyer's wife. Well, I guess widow now. We met at your husband's funeral. Fancy, us meeting again. And at another funeral."

"Yes. Fancy," said the other woman, though she did not sound like she fancied it at all.

"Do you want me to tell you about the body?" chirped Mary Beth, trying to restart the conversation.

"God, no!" said Lisa, looking positively green at the thought.

Mary Beth looked crushed. She had such a pivotal role in a crime, and no one wanted to know about it. "What do you do, for, you know, a job?" asked Mary Beth, at one last attempt to make conversation.

"I'm run an art gallery, in New York," replied Lisa.

"New York?" enthused Mary Beth. "Oh, that is so cool. I am, like, so jealous. I would love to live in New York. I, like, go there all the time."

Lisa nodded, without much enthusiasm.

"Don't you love New York?" asked Mary Beth.

"Well, I was thinking of moving, but now with all that has happened, I guess I'll stay." Lisa excused herself quietly, walked to the pew three rows back and sat down again.

*****

"What a great service," sighed C.J. contentedly. "I'm a little sad I didn't know Jeffie did so much for the community. He seems a little like a stranger now. Why is it that everyone has to have a secret in life?"

"I don't have any secrets," said Betsy, virtuously.

"None at all? Not a single one?"

Betsy thought for a moment, and remembered the new and rather expensive sewing machine she had bought last year without telling her husband. "Well, almost none."

C.J., now curious, was about to press Betsy on her secret, when Walter stumbled towards them. "Dear God!" he exclaimed. "I am going home to immerse myself in a bath of disinfectant. I have been touched by at least four homeless people, and I swear one of them was trying to steal my wallet. And just now, some pasty lady who needed to go on a diet fifteen dress sizes ago tried to offer me a casserole. Do I look like the type of man who eats casseroles?"

"Oh! Are they serving the food now?" cried C.J., ignoring Walter's complaints. "I am so darn excited. I don't mean that I'm not sad about Jeffie. But I am as hungry as a pig at dawn, and I spied some good ole mac'n'cheese and green beans'n'fried onions and something with marshmallow fluff on top. Just like the potlucks back home. Y'all excuse me, I got to grab a plate before it's all gone."

C.J. found herself in the food line behind the Reverend Jackson. She tapped him on the shoulder to get his attention. When the Reverend spotted the hot pink cowboy boots accenting the black mourning dress, he certainly couldn't help but notice C.J.

"Excuse me, Reverend. I'm a work colleague of Jefferson's. C.J. Whitmore is the name." With this, C.J. stuck out her hand, and Tayshon shook it firmly. "I just wanted to thank you for today. I really liked Jeffie, and that was a mighty fine way to remember him," said C.J.

"Well, thank you, Ms. Whitmore," said Tayshon, oozing politeness.

"Professor," corrected C.J. automatically. C.J. didn't know if Tayshon had mistaken her for a secretary or just hadn't thought to use her title. But C.J. wished she hadn't corrected the earnest, young minister. It sounded so pedantic and officious to care about her title outside the world of academia. Especially as she didn't know if she was using his title correctly. Did he prefer Reverend Jackson? Just plain Reverend? She had no idea.

"Sorry?" asked Tayshon, confused.

"It's nothing. Please, call me C.J."

"Of course. C.J. it is."

C.J., terrible at small talk, was now stuck for something to say. The problem with meeting someone at a funeral is that the one person you have in common is, unfortunately, dead. "So, you knew Jeffie well it seems."

"Yes. He was a regular here at St. Andrews."

C.J. searched the recesses of her mind for another topic of conversation. She could bring up the homeless who seemed to be wandering about the church, but C.J. had become an economist so she didn't have to experience poverty. God wasn't going to be a conversation starter, as C.J. and the Lord weren't on speaking terms. It seemed Jefferson was the safest bet. "Did you know Jeffie was planning to move to New Mexico?"

The Reverend Jackson looked thoughtful. "Yes. I did."

C.J. looked at him. "You look so serious about it. I mean, I wouldn't choose alpaca farming, either. I know what it's like to ranch animals. That's what I grew up doing. You know, I said to my friend Betsy, 'I'll bet you ten dollars that he doesn't even last one year out there.' But," C.J. looked sad, "now we'll never know."

Tayshon looked at her sadly. "I counseled him not to go. Perhaps that is why he changed his..." The Reverend stopped in mid-sentence.

"Why he changed his what?" asked C.J., confused. "His mind? He wasn't planning on going after all?"

"It is of no importance. The Lord will always provide."

C.J. gave the Reverend a long look. "You know, I like a mystery as much as a chicken likes an axe. The Lord will always provide what? Money? Had Jeffie told you that he was leaving money to your church in his will?"

Tayshon looked uncomfortable. "Well, yes. We had talked about it at length. He had no family and wanted to leave the church as his sole beneficiary."

"Well, that makes sense. I wonder when he changed his mind. What did you say when you counseled him to not go to New Mexico?"

Tayshon looked C.J. straight in the eyes. "I said that happiness cannot be built on pain."

*****

As C.J. and Betsy were sitting enjoying their mac and cheese, Mary Beth came up and joined them.

C.J. took one glance at the Halloween apparition before her and exploded. "Oh, Mother of Gooseberries, what is on your head, girl? And take that damn veil off. You aren't his widow of fifty years. You were his secretary. Keep it in perspective."

Betsy kept her napkin to her lips, trying to suppress the giggles.

Mary Beth looked huffy. "I took extra care with my outfit. I am, after all, the Discoverer of the Body. I was a little surprised that I wasn't mentioned in the service."

C.J. stared at her. "Yeah. Me too. Darn. Maybe next time."

Mary Beth perked up. "You're right, Professor Whitmore. You always look on the bright side. Maybe next time."

Betsy knew C.J. was about to point out in none-too-kind words that if there were a next time it was likely to be Mary Beth who was killed. By her. So she piped up. "You know, Mary Beth, there were so many people here. It's so wonderful to see Jefferson loved by so many. C.J. and I were trying to work out who we saw from the department. We saw Walter, and we think we glimpsed Peter cowering at the back of the church. I am sure I saw Charles and Mildred in the middle of the action, and C.J. swears she saw the President of the College doing a butt bump with a hefty African-American woman, but I think she's pulling my leg. Did you see anyone?"

"Not from the department. But I did see Edmund's wife. Well, I guess she's his widow now."

"Lisa is here?" asked C.J. "I am sorry I missed her. How is she doing?"

"You know, it's funny. She looked pretty upset. And when I offered to tell her about the body to distract her, she looked like she was going to puke. Anyway, I don't know why she's so worked up. Her husband died, like, days ago. And she didn't even live with him. She lives in New York. And you know what? She told me she had been thinking of leaving New York. I guess to come up here and live with Professor DeBeyer. And now she doesn't have to. She can stay in New York. If I was her, I wouldn't be crying. I would be, like, so happy."

MONDAY

No longer a media darling, Knollwood Place was once again a calm memorial to grander times. The oak trees were gracefully losing their leaves. The grand houses of yesteryear stood proudly, only slightly marred by the signs that stood before them announcing the likes of "Economics Department" and "Microeconomics Research Center." Those waiting in line for the chili truck were now only the hung-over and hungry, instead of the people hungry for those who would be hung.

Charles Covington III ambled down the street to his small office at 41 Knollwood. *No*, he thought, *I don't know if anyone would think this is the most magnificent street in America any more. But, it sure is beautiful to me.*

Charles was feeling much more relaxed since attending young Jefferson's funeral the day before. As he and Mildred were getting ready to leave the rather lively affair, they had run into C.J.

"Charles, can I speak to you a moment?"

Truth be told, Charles had been rather tired and ready to head home, but, of course, he didn't like to refuse a lady. He excused himself from Mildred and stepped outside with C.J. where they could hear themselves talk.

"You should tell Mildred everything," C.J. said, meaningfully. "And the sooner the better."

Charles looked at her in surprise. "You mean, you know?"

"Yes. I know."

"About..."

"Yes. And Mildred needs to know, too. It will be fine. Trust me."

Charles whistled a little ditty to himself as he walked towards his office. That little Texas rose had been right. He should have told Mildred years ago. No good keeping secrets. It lands you in all sorts of trouble.

When he arrived at his office, Charles eased himself into his desk chair and opened his email. Such a fascinating concept, email. Little letters being sent instantly across the world.

Charles still remembered the time of no computers, followed by the years when the faculty had all used one central computer, booking time to use it. In those days, he used punch cards to write code, and (though he didn't tell very many people this story), he published a paper with completely erroneous results as he had entered the punch cards backwards into the computer. Charles hadn't realized the error until years later. Now, everything was at his desk—the computer, the printer and the scanner. It was so very, very clever.

Charles perused his inbox. Oh...the pumpkin carving competition sounded interesting. He and Mildred should go. And there was a message from C.J. What did she want?

Charles opened the email.

FROM: C.J. Whitmore
TO: All faculty, All staff, All graduate students
SUBJECT: Seminar today ... who dunnit?

Good morning!

As you know, we have lost two of our colleagues recently to murder. I now know who killed both

Edmund and Jefferson and will explain everything at the start of Peter's seminar this afternoon at two o'clock, if he will kindly indulge me a few minutes.

C.J.

Well, well. He wasn't surprised that C.J. had worked things out. She was a bright one. And gentle on the eyes to boot. Charles changed his afternoon plans. He was definitely going to the seminar. This was going to be very interesting.

*****

The graduate students in Jefferson's class were sitting around, waiting for whoever was going to come and teach them.

"Please, don't let it be Professor Scovill," said one student.

"What's wrong with Walt Wit-less?" asked another, dryly.

"Maybe there's still time to accept the offer I got from Cornell," joked Jose.

Snickers broke out around the room. It would take a natural disaster on a gargantuan scale to get any of these self-assured graduate students to set foot inside Cornell. They were, after all, Eaton-quality.

"Oh, my God!" Annika exclaimed loudly, breaking the mood. She was staring wide-eyed at her smart phone.

The room fell silent. It was unlike Annika to make a fuss.

"What's wrong?" asked Jose.

"This email, from Professor Whitmore. She says she knows who the murderer is, and she is going to tell all at Professor Johansson's seminar this afternoon."

A cacophony of commentaries flooded this announcement.

"She does not."

"Maybe I'll finally win the betting pool."

"I reckon it's been Professor Choi the whole time."

"Who's willing to take an even money bet on Professor Scovill?"

"Well, I'm going to seminar. Try and stop me."

Annika looked over at Jose. He was sitting silently in his chair, looking very thoughtful.

*****

Yesterday's memorial service did not remind Walter that life was short. It reminded him that a large portion of the population lived in poverty, hence the invention of gated communities. Despite showering twice the previous night and once again this morning, Walter was still applying generous amounts of Purell. He did not want to catch the poverty virus.

Walter opened his email, saw that he had 56 new messages and so closed it again. Whatever the complaining masses wanted, it would have to wait. He couldn't deal with the whims of the fretting minions now. He had to go and teach Jefferson's class.

*****

Mary Beth was disappointed with the funeral for Professor Daniels. There had been, like, no focus on her. She might as well have not found his body, for all it was worth. And, to make matters worse, there was no rich husband material in sight at that church. It was swarming with poor people, ugly people, old people and gay people. No one she needed to waste her time on. At least Professor DeBeyer had attracted a small, select group of elite mourners. That's what you really wanted at a funeral.

Mary Beth attacked the computer keys with unusual vigor. She had waxed, plucked, dyed and dermed every pore of her body and just buried the best chance she had of Mr. Rich. It would be a foolish person who asked for a large photocopy job today. Pretending to do work, Mary Beth clicked on her email.

Nordstrom's sale.

"And so they should. It'll bring their prices down to reasonable."

Ten percent off at Macy's.

"Not exciting. Every day is sale day at Macy's"

Shoe sale at Bergdorf's.

"Oh, now that's interesting. A pair of fall boots would lift the spirits."

Mary Beth was planning her shopping trip to New York when she clicked open C.J.'s email. Why would C.J. send her an email about a seminar? She was, like, totally not interested in economics. "Oh!" cried Mary Beth, to no one in particular. "C.J. knows who the murderer is!"

*****

Stephen sat at his desk. Not that it was going to be his desk for much longer. He had emailed the Dean his letter of resignation that morning. He had no intention of dragging out his time at Eaton University, like an aging football star past his prime. This way, Stephen thought, he could at least leave quickly and not suffer through the surreptitious glances, the veiled questions about his "plans," and the humiliation of sitting through job market seminars for his job.

Stephen knew he was done with academia. One arrest, however false, would besmirch a reputation forever. No. Stephen Choi was going to turn his life upside down. Live where he wanted. Do what he wanted. In fact, do something he dreamed of doing as a child. Expectations be damned.

He googled "Fireman Training Hawaii." His search returned "Honolulu Community College."

"What exactly is a community college?" wondered Stephen. Such institutions were mentioned frequently in

State of the Union addresses when presidents were trying to bolster faltering education policies, but Stephen could never remember meeting anyone who attended one. He searched around the website of Honolulu Community College. Small class sizes. Specialized curriculum.

Hmmm, thought Stephen. *It sounds rather elite. I hope I get in.* As Stephen started working up an elaborate, pre-application letter, he noticed he had new mail in his inbox.

*****

"Is it true?" Betsy asked breathlessly, as she arrived at Wallaby's coffee shop. She had clearly been walking faster than was comfortable—her face was flushed red and her chest was heaving.

"Betsy!" exclaimed C.J. "Please, you need to take a seat."

Betsy lowered her bulk into a seat but wasn't to be distracted. "Is it true?" she asked again, her tone more urgent.

"Is what true?" asked C.J., rather cruelly, as she knew exactly what Betsy was referring to.

"I just read your email. Do you know who the murderer is?"

"I do," said C.J., enjoying the feeling of stringing out her friend. "I finally worked it out last night."

"Well, don't just sit there. Tell me! Who is it?"

C.J. placed her hand on her friend's shoulder. "I thought the email was clear. I am going to explain it to everyone at the start of Peter's seminar at two o'clock today."

Betsy groaned. "You are the most infuriating woman, you know that? You aren't Hercule Poirot, waiting for the great unveiling. Just spill it."

"Actually," said C.J. "I do feel a bit like Hercule. Though not as stylish or foreign. But now I understand why he called everyone together and told his story so dramatically. He didn't want to have to keep repeating himself, and neither do I. Two o'clock."

Betsy looked crushed. Then she asked quietly, "Is it someone we know?"

"Betsy!" reprimanded C.J. "You can't get the information that way. But, yes. It is someone you know."

"I knew it!" cried Betsy excitedly. She waited for a moment. "Is it an economist?"

"Betsy," C.J.'s voice held a strong tone of warning. Then, after a few seconds she said, "Yes."

"Hah!" Betsy was triumphant. The large woman was quiet for a long time, thinking how to formulate her next question. "Is the murderer a male?"

C.J. looked at her friend in surprise. "Betsy, if you are trying to ask if I, the lone tenured female on staff, killed Edmund and Jefferson, the answer is no. So thus, yes, the killer is a male."

Betsy looked sheepish. "Sorry. Just had to check."

The pair was quiet again. C.J. was enjoying her coffee. Betsy was deep in thought.

Suddenly, Betsy looked up. "Oh my God. It's Walter, isn't it. Walter is the killer. I have always thought there was something off about that man. There's just something a little...odd about him. It is, isn't it? You can tell me. It's Walter...isn't it?"

C.J. finished her coffee, gathered her purse and looked Betsy straight in the face. "I hope you can come to seminar at two. Because I will reveal who is responsible for the murders then."

"But, but...what if the killer murders you in the meantime? To stop you from talking. Shouldn't you tell someone as an insurance policy?"

C.J. smiled. "I'm from Texas. I can look after myself just fine."

*****

For once, there were no stragglers into the seminar room. On this Monday, at least, research into people's preferences for blue cars over red cars or the optimal number of Starbuck stores in New York City had not been deemed too urgent to prevent the faculty from attending the seminar. The room was full to the point of overflowing. Most of the graduate students, including Annika and Jose, were wedged into the back of the room. The faculty from 41 and 43 Knollwood had crossed the road for the event, and the esteemed colleagues from 40 and 42 Knollwood were on time, with their laptops closed.

Walter, having finally condescended to read his email after the morning graduate class, was pacing up and down in front of the room. That Texan…hussy. She didn't have the right to call a faculty meeting or muscle in on a seminar. By Article Seven of the by-laws, only the Chair of the department could do that. He was going to tell her what he thought of her high-handed ways. Maybe this was a sufficient violation to get her tenure revoked.

But, Walter thought grimly, *that was highly unlikely. Affirmative action and women's rights and all that.*

Regardless, he wasn't going to stand for this. He, Walter, controlled this department.

Charles was sitting at the front, hearing aids turned up high. No doubt about it. This was going to be a humdinger of a show. Mildred, God bless her, was waiting at home with the G&T's on ice, ready to hear all about it.

Stephen was skulking at the back of the room, hidden amongst the graduate students. He didn't get a Ph.D. for nothing. He understood that a fair number of his colleagues thought he had killed both men, even though he was out of the state when Jefferson had died.

Did C.J. really know who the killer was? He sure hoped so.

Betsy had snared a seat towards the middle of the room, having cancelled her afternoon class. As an adjunct she knew that she was expected to sit at the back of the room for a seminar, but she didn't care. Betsy had been following this drama since the day it started and wanted to be able to see all the major players. The ruffled egos would have to cope.

Mary Beth, overcome with curiosity, had thought she would slip in and watch the proceedings. However, Walter spied her as she came into the room. Unable to control C.J., he wasn't going to let this transgression of rank go unnoticed. "Do you want something Mary Beth?" he asked acidly.

"Uh, no?" she answered, uncertain of what to say. She wanted a seat, but she was pretty sure Professor Scovill wasn't offering her one. He was using his mean voice.

"Were you planning on sharing your astute and erudite comments on Professor Johannson's seminar?" Walter asked snidely.

"Um, well, I'm not sure..." Mary Beth faltered. She didn't know what "astute" or "erudite" meant, so it was hard to say.

"Then I suggest you get back to your photocopy machine where you belong."

The rest of the faculty was waiting impatiently. The atmosphere in the room was tense, quiet and edgy. Throats were cleared. Legs were crossed and uncrossed. Smart phones were unattended, like unloved children abandoned in a parking lot. The department had lived under the cloud of a killer for too long. They were more than ready for it to end.

C.J. strode in at three minutes after two, dressed much as she had been the first day she came to work after receiving tenure. Pink cowboy boots, turquoise skirt, and, today, she had finished the ensemble with an orange-spangled cowgirl shirt.

"Well, a full house and it's only a few minutes after two. I feel flattered, gentlemen." C.J. turned to Walter, who was still pacing at the front of the room. "You see, you can get them to arrive on time. You just have to kill a few of them off first."

Walter closed his eyes. Babies. All women left work to have babies.

"Walt," said C.J. in a friendly tone, "go rest your patootie. This is going to take some time."

Walter remained standing, glared, and finally, reluctantly, took the only seat available, a folding chair at the back of the room vacated for him by a graduate student. He would deal with this outrage later.

C.J. turned to Peter, whose seminar she had hijacked. "Thanks for the loan of the seminar."

Peter nervously ran his hand over his scalp and then nodded his head in acknowledgement. He couldn't actually remember being given the opportunity to turn her down.

C.J. then turned to address the room. "We all know why we are here today. Two of our own have been killed, and we want to know who is responsible. That person may be sitting right here amongst us now."

People glanced around surreptitiously at their neighbors.

"Oh please, don't try and be subtle. We've thought of nothing else since this started. Which one of us is the killer? For a bunch of supposedly bright Ph.D.'s, we should be able to work it out. It's just a case of being able to pick the lemon."

Charles cleared his throat. "Young lady, what are you talking about? What lemon? Why are we talking about fruit?"

"Charles, have you ever bought a used car?"

Charles nodded. "Oh yes. A fine 1965 Ford Mustang. Picked that baby up for just over a grand. What a car." Charles sighed at the memory.

C.J. smiled. "So, it was a good car?"

"A good car?" Charles sounded almost affronted at this faint praise. "It was a dream on four wheels."

"That's great to hear. How did you know it was a good car when you bought it?"

"What do you mean, how did I know? I know about cars. I looked under the hood and test drove it. It was, obviously, a great car."

Betsy followed this exchange with interest. What was C.J. doing? Why was she trapping Charles into her lemon theory? Was she proving that Charles was a murderer after all?

C.J. was still focused on Charles. "Charles, have you ever bought a second-hand car that turned out to be a dog?"

Charles squirmed in his seat. "Well, I guess. It happens."

"Of course it happens," C.J. enthused. "It's happened to us all. What happened in your case?"

"It was a 1970 Plymouth Fury. Cherry red. Must'a been in an accident or something before I bought it. Because that thing just never drove right."

"Thank you, Charles, for illustrating my point. Your Plymouth Fury was a lemon, but it was hard to know that because the seller didn't tell you all the information. Our challenge here today is that we have a bunch of good people in this room, and we want to pick the lemon—the murderer."

Charles nodded his head in understanding, as did many of the other faculty. It had been many years since they had thought about any economic problem other than their own research agenda. It was good to get a refresher course.

"Now, this is an easy model to solve in theoretical economics land, where everyone is rational and behaves as they should." Here C.J. cast a disparaging glance over towards Walter. "But you folks are astonishingly irrational, highly emotional, and, I have to say, very secretive. You may not be murderers, but you have a lot of other crap going on that you don't want people to know about. Which means you behave like a lemon, even if you didn't kill anyone at all."

Stephen decided he didn't need to put himself through this and started to ease himself to the door.

C.J. snapped her fingers at him and pointed him back into the room. "So, if you are all ready, let's start at the beginning, and sort this mess out.

"This all started with the death of Edmund DeBeyer, a man strangled in his office by his own Ph.D. hood. An office located in the fourteenth most violent city in America. Was this fact important? No. The violence of Elm Grove is gun violence and drive-by shootings. Edmund died a very personal, un-premeditated death. It was clear he knew his killer. This ruled out the students, as Edmund would never have a personal relationship with a student. Too demeaning. His ego demanded glamorous relationships, like that with his young, beautiful and successful wife, Lisa. Besides, we all would have heard if Edmund was sleeping with a student. The Eaton University rumor mill would have taken care of that."

C.J. cast a meaningful glance in Walter's direction. Did he really think they all didn't know about his assignations with the blonde, ponytail club?

"A stranger would have arrived armed with a motive to rob or terrorize the professor in some way. But this, this did not happen. Professor DeBeyer was strangled with a weapon of opportunity. So we have our first pieces of key information. The killer must have been one of us or his wife."

Again, the faculty began looking around, evaluating each other as potential killers.

"It was easy to rule out Lisa DeBeyer. She was at her gallery in New York all day, seen by many clients and staff. She could not have driven up to Elm Grove, killed Edmund and driven back. She would have been missed for that amount of time. Similarly, many of the faculty were also accounted for in the hour before Edmund's death. They were teaching, like Peter here, or in Maui or some other idyllic location." C.J. raised an eyebrow in the direction of her vacationing colleagues.

"But not all. We could not account for Stephen Choi, Walter Scovill, Jefferson Daniels, Charles Covington III, and, of course, myself."

Stephen shrank back even further into his seat. Charles looked intensely interested in where C.J. was taking this line of reasoning. Walter began to object vociferously. "Hey. What are you playing at? I did not kill the man. And I will not have any suggestion made that I did."

The rest of the faculty looked much more cheerful now. Clearly, they were off the hook. It was either Stephen, Walter or Charles and, frankly, given his age, unlikely to be Charles. So that left Stephen or Walter. Given the last outburst, odds were clearly in favor of it being Walter.

"Mary Beth provided us with one further piece of the puzzle," continued C.J., ignoring Walter. "We were initially told Edmund died within an hour of our finding him at just after two o'clock. However, Mary Beth overheard an argument occurring in Edmund's office at approximately one-fifteen. This argument could have been over the phone or in person, but it was indicative that the murder may have taken place at approximately that time.

"At first, we all looked at Stephen as the suspect. The police arrested him the day after the murder. We all know there is no smoke without a fire. What evidence did they have? What had he done?"

Stephen, at the back of the room, was making himself as small as possible.

C.J. noticed this. "Stephen honey, don't hide back there. Come on down."

Stephen didn't move.

"He's just like a cat I once had," C.J. observed. "So shy, but lovely once you got to know him. Anyway, we all knew Stephen hated Edmund. Blamed him for not getting tenure, though, Stephen darling, if we are being honest, you were never getting tenure. Your publication rate was well below par. And all those trips home to Asia. There is a time and place to see Mom, and it is not while you are a junior professor."

Murmurs of agreement went around the room. C.J. was gutsy and had said what others did not want to say to Stephen.

"But, the strange thing was that on the day of the murder, Stephen said he was in his office in the hours before the seminar. But he wasn't. He was away from the building. Mary Beth saw him going downtown at about one o'clock and getting back after two. In his office, he could have ducked out and killed Edmund. Away from the building, in downtown Elm Grove, he had a perfect alibi. So why hide it?"

C.J. left the question hanging. "Tell me Stephen, on your trips to Asia, did you even go to Korea to see your mother, or did you go straight to Macau?"

Stephen just shook his head, unwilling to answer.

"Stephen isn't a killer, he's a recovering gambler. That explains the trips to Macau. The lack of time devoted to his research. The erratic swings in temper... sometimes very confident after a win, sometimes down and depressed. A little statistics knowledge and a great intelligence can be a dangerous combination. On Monday, between one and two, there is a Gamblers Anonymous meeting in town. Out of respect to the code of anonymity which Stephen tried so hard to follow, I won't say where."

Stephen finally spoke. "It's true. I have a gambling problem. I was so angry at Edmund for not getting tenure, I felt I could have killed him, but I just started going to GA meetings and am learning to accept that the responsibility is mine. It, um, doesn't happen at once." He laughed ruefully. "I came back that afternoon and started to write a letter of apology to everyone in the department. I am really sorry I didn't give you all my full commitment and effort while I was here. It was a great privilege to work with you all."

An uncomfortable silence settled on the room. Most of the faculty had been so sure the young man had been a killer. Yet all this time, he had needed their help.

Charles asked, "What are you going to do now, son?"

"Well, that is the question, isn't it? Everyone said that I was so smart I could have everything...well, I tried for everything, and now, I have nothing. So maybe, I need to think in a different dimension. I've applied to a program in Hawaii. To learn to be a fireman," he ended with a self-conscious laugh.

If Stephen hadn't been studying his shoes so intently, he would have noticed some of the faculty looked rather envious. Betsy teared up with pride and smiled in his direction. If only people realized how important it was to do what they enjoyed doing. Forty years was a long time to fulfill someone else's expectations.

C.J. nodded reassuringly to Stephen and gave him a wink. Then she continued. "So, if it wasn't Stephen, then who was it? My personal favorite was Jefferson. He had the physical strength and he had the opportunity. Sure, he was out running, but it wouldn't take more than a few minutes to pop in and do the deed. Mary Beth could not be certain what time she saw him come in from the run, because her new analog watch was proving so confusing. It could have been ten past one or one-fifty. If it was the former, Jefferson had plenty of time to commit the crime and could have been the person Edmund was heard arguing with at about a quarter past one.

"Furthermore, putting all the evidence of everyone's movements together, it seems more probable that it was ten past one when Mary Beth saw Jeffie. Mary Beth said she saw Jefferson come in before she saw Annika leave and Annika thinks she left 40 Knollwood at one-forty that day. So, it seems more likely that Jefferson came in at one-ten.

"But did he have a reason to kill Edmund? I could imagine that if you spent that much time with Edmund, the urge to do him in would come eventually. Charles said money was the most powerful motive, and Edmund and Jefferson were favored to win the Nobel. I happened upon a letter that indicated that Edmund was systematically ruining Jefferson's career and, therefore, Jefferson's chance of sharing in the Nobel and its million plus prize money. That seemed like a financial motive and fit with Jefferson being the killer. But, then, Jefferson resigned to become an alpaca farmer. This meant Jefferson wasn't motivated by his career or money after all. And then, tragically, Jefferson himself was killed, removing him completely from the suspect list.

"So then, my friend," said C.J., turning to Walter, "there was you. Again, there were the lies. You told the police and all that would listen that you were in your office between one and two."

"That isn't a lie," cried Walter. "That is exactly where I was."

The faculty was at full attention. Betsy couldn't wait to tell her friends in quilting group about today. This was proving far more interesting than any T.V. crime drama. Stephen, relieved from suspicion and the burden of secrets, was quite relaxed from his position at the back of the room.

"Walter, the problem when we start to lie is there are so many little cracks where the truth starts to leak through. That is the great thing about data. It cannot help but be heard. On the day of Edmund's murder, Jose Grimaldo made a study date with Annika Jonsdottir in the Smythe Lounge at one-thirty. It turns out that Annika's movements that day were important not only in placing a time on Jefferson's movements, they helped elucidate yours too.

"Now Annika, being the studious girl she is, got to the Smythe Lounge early. Also hoping that it would be a little more than a study date, if you get my drift, she set up her books in the darkest, most remote corner, where she could see if anyone, namely one, handsome Jose, entered, but no one would notice them. At about one-fifteen, she saw Professor Walter Scovill come into the Smythe Lounge from the 42 Knollwood side, cross the room, and go through to 40 Knollwood Place. She thought nothing of it at the time. Ten, maybe fifteen minutes passed. Professor Walter Scovill comes back through the Smythe Lounge and goes back to 42 Knollwood, presumably back to his office. Annika isn't thinking anything about Professor Scovill, but is only thinking of Jose. She waits fifteen more minutes, but no Jose arrives. Too upset to go to the seminar, she goes back to her dorm room. Mary Beth can attest that she saw Annika, leaving 40 Knollwood, crying, some time before two."

C.J. paused her story.

Charles harrumphed into his mustache.

If anyone had looked at the back of the room, they would have noticed that Jose had turned very pale.

Walter blustered. "You are going to believe the word of a sniveling graduate student, against me, a world famous Eaton University Professor? This is outrageous."

"Now, when Annika came to me, she was afraid you had committed the murder. But, as I had already witnessed your...shoe shine...I was not so sure. When Annika asked Jose where he was, he said he was late paying student fees and was detained. Student fees, I thought. That is very interesting. Jose is a full-scholarship student. So I made a few calls. Jose didn't owe any student fees. Jose didn't have any outstanding library loans. Jose didn't owe anyone any money. But Jose had been given a Howard Foundation Grant that had not been approved by the committee. Just by one Professor Walter Scovill.

"I asked Jose about it, Professor Scovill."

"Now we're believing the story of a Mexcian field rat?" yelled Walter.

"What story, Walter? What do you think Jose said?" asked C.J. coolly.

"My private life is none of your business."

"But...what shall we call it...indentured servitude is my business. I think Charles can fill us in on the history of servitude in this country. Charles, when did the first indentured servants come across to America?"

Charles cleared his throat. "Well now, the Virginia Company was the first to use them. They brought across laborers to America in the early 17th century. In exchange for passage, the indentured servants had to work for about five years."

"And when did it end?" asked C.J.

Charles pursed his lips in concentration. "Well, of course, it is hard to pin point the exact date it ended, but it has been gone about a hundred years."

C.J. leveled her gaze at Walter. "Do you want to tell everyone what you were doing between one-fifteen and one-thirty on the day Edmund was murdered?"

Anger oozed out of Walter. "I was in my office," he said, in carefully measured tones.

C.J. turned her gaze to Jose. "Jose, what were you doing at one-fifteen on the day Edmund was murdered?"

Jose rose to his feet slowly. In a quiet, steady voice he said, "At Professor Scovill's request, I waited for him in the men's bathroom in the basement of 40 Knollwood. Professor Scovill met me there to give me the keys to his car and instructions for the afternoon. I noticed he liked to vary the places we met. I think he didn't want to draw attention to the fact I had to meet with him so often.

"On that day, I was to drive the car to his house, wash his car and his wife's car, and detail the inside of each car as well. Also, there was some yard work he wanted done. When I started in the program at Eaton University, Professor Scovill informed me that to keep my place in the program and my scholarship funding I was required to be at his beck and call for the duration of my time at Eaton University, doing whatever manual work he required."

The seminar room was absolutely quiet. Betsy was thinking of the suffering Jose had endured. Charles was debating the merits of indentured servitude as a system of recruiting a labor force. The senior faculty was mulling over the scandal this was going to create. The negative publicity of having the Chair of the department indenture a graduate student. It was going to be horrific. Harvard was going to have a field day with this.

C.J. asked, "What sort of work have you done for Professor Scovill since you started at Eaton University?"

"Well, I have washed his cars and polished his shoes. I rake his yard and shovel his snow. I do other yard work, like hedging. I have helped Mrs. Scovill with housework. It just depends on what needs doing."

C.J. turned her attention back to Walter. "I don't think you are the killer, but I do think the time for indentured servitude has past. As Charles said, the practice ended in this country one hundred years ago. Because I have trained my students to collect data at all times, I have in my possession an email with details of your exploitations, with times and pictures. So I think you will excuse us if we choose to believe the story of a …what was the charming phrase you used…a Mexican field rat? Just as an FYI, that "field rat" is an extremely intelligent, personable young man whose name is Jose."

Jose felt Annika squeezing his hand. Walter, who had turned chalk white with rage, glared from his chair at the back of the room in silence. This was not going to end here.

C.J. continued as if nothing had happened. "But of course, we still have a killer. It could be Charles, with his ladder."

Charles perked up at hearing his name.

"Goodness knows that Charles had a college try at being the killer. Even confessing to the crime and spending some time in the city jail. But, it turned out, that Charles had his own reasons for this, and it wasn't him."

Charles stood up. "Now, now. That isn't much of an explanation. How are folks going to know what was really going on? I am not ashamed of the reason I confessed. It's nice of you to want to let me keep my secrets, but they aren't secrets any more now that Mildred knows."

C.J. smiled. "I'm glad to hear it Charles."

"I 'fessed up to that scoundrel Edmund's murder because I wanted people to stop asking me where I was on the day he died. I was with my daughter, Charlotte."

There was a lot of murmuring around the room. Mildred and Charles did not have any children.

"You don't have to whisper. Charlotte isn't Mildred's daughter. I was unfaithful to dear Mildred about 20 odd years ago. A stupid mistake. I was sixty-something acting like I was sixteen. And with a woman thirty years younger than me. Don't know what I was thinking, when I have the sweetest wife in the world at home. But, now there is dear Charlotte. She is an undergraduate here at Eaton University. Such a bright, dear thing. I didn't want to hurt Mildred and have her find out. I thought it would be better to be a murderer than be a cheating husband."

Charles looked down, tears brimming in his eyes. "But my darling Mildred. I didn't expect Mildred to forgive me, but she has. Charlotte's mother passed away several years ago, and Mildred has enough love for me and Charlotte. I have never been so happy as I am now, as I can share my two favorite women with each other and the world."

C.J. patted Charles on the shoulder as the old man sat down.

"But how did you know?" Charles asked C.J., as an afterthought.

"Charlotte is in Edmund's class, which I got stuck teaching. The physical resemblance between the two of you is striking, which raised my suspicions. Then, when I complimented her on her excellent economic skills, she said she took after her father. Once she began to make connections to historical economies in her questions in class, it just confirmed what I already knew. I realized, after foolishly checking her last name on the student list, that it was her father's first name that she had. Charles. Charlotte."

Charles just harrumphed into his mustache.

"But you had me going for a while with the ladder Charles. I kept thinking that it gave everyone access to the room. But then I realized that because the killer was one of us, the easiest way to get access to Edmund's room without creating a scene was through the door. We all go in and out of each other's offices all day. No one would even notice if a colleague was coming from Edmund's office. But they would notice if one was scaling a ladder. The ladder didn't help at all."

"I was just getting the leaves off the roof," Charles said, somewhat confused.

"I know," C.J. agreed. "Well, getting back to the murder of Edmund, it could have been me. But I have data for the parking meters for the entire two hours leading up to the killing. So, I look like a poor candidate. Did Edmund strangle himself? It seems it must be the case, looking at the facts for the first murder. We seem to have a murder in which all of the possible suspects are accounted for.

"So we turn to the second murder. Jefferson Daniels was found poisoned in his office. The difficulty with Jefferson's murder is that the cyanide was in a full container of protein powder. Therefore, Jefferson had just started to use this container. The cyanide could have been sitting in the container for weeks without him knowing. The poison could have been put in the protein powder at any time, by any one. No one could have an alibi.

"So now we have two murders, one no one could have done, and one everyone could have done," C.J. concluded. "I have to tell you, I was completely baffled, until Jefferson's memorial service. It was when Mary Beth said that Lisa DeBeyer was at the funeral and that she wasn't moving away any more that I understood why both Edmund and Jefferson were killed.

"My biggest problem was that I been making a fundamental mistake in my assumptions. I was assuming the same person had killed both Edmund and Jefferson. But actually, there was nothing to indicate that this was true. The method of death was very different. Would one person be an impulsive strangler and a careful, planned poisoner? I realized I needed to relax this assumption and allow for two different killers.

"Charles had said to follow the money and we would solve the crime. In a way, he was right. The two murders weren't about money. But the money was the clue. The murders were about love. The love triangle of Edmund, Jefferson and Lisa."

The faculty looked uncomfortably around at each other. Love? In the land of economics? It was so... unseemly.

"The money was a big clue in this crime. The day Edmund's will was read out, he showed his hand. He didn't leave any money to his wife. He constructed a research institute that was inaccessible to Jefferson. His will wasn't about how much he loved himself. It was about how much he hated Lisa and Jeffie. Jefferson's will had recently been changed to make Edmund and Lisa the beneficiaries, instead of the church of St. Andrews. Jefferson had changed his will to make sure

Lisa benefitted, giving away how much he loved her. As they say, money talks.

"Now we understand the motivation, the story falls into place. Edmund and Jefferson worked so closely together. Edmund's wife was much closer in age to the handsome, charismatic Jefferson. It was only natural that her affections would shift over. And what about her wouldn't Jefferson love? She is a beautiful, talented, artistic woman. Now so many little details made sense. Jefferson's resignation for one. He and Lisa were planning on moving to Santa Fe, New Mexico together. She was going to set up her art gallery, he was going to give up economics for her. So of course, at Jefferson's funeral, Lisa wasn't planning to move anymore. The pastor at St. Andrews knew all about the plans and counseled Jefferson against it. He told Jefferson that happiness could not be built on pain. It seems that the Reverend is a very wise man.

"Some time before the day of Edmund's murder, Lisa must have told Edmund she was leaving him for Jefferson. To someone of Edmund's self-importance, this would have been galling. His ego would not have been able to take this calmly. He wanted it all—the Nobel prize, the beautiful wife…and he wasn't going to let an upstart like Jefferson Daniels take anything that belonged to him.

"On the day of the murder, Edmund was methodically enacting his revenge. He was sending out letters to the Nobel committee saying Jefferson had only being a research assistant and all their work was Edmund's alone. When they left morning coffee together, I can guarantee Edmund took great pleasure in telling Jefferson his plans. Jefferson left for his run but couldn't stop thinking about it. At just after one o'clock, Jefferson stopped his run short and went up to Edmund's office to reason with him. Mary Beth overheard their argument. Edmund told Jefferson that he was 'finished.' I think we can extrapolate to the type of threats that went along with this. Jefferson was never going to have Lisa. He was going to kill both of them first. Jefferson's career was over. And other such pleasantries. Jefferson, consumed with rage and the need to protect Lisa and everything he had worked for, strangled Edmund. It was, indeed, a crime of passion."

The room was silent.

Finally, Charles spoke up. "That poor bugger, Jefferson. And then he killed himself. That bastard Edmund has a lot to answer for."

"Well, maybe more than you think. The tearful Jefferson we saw around the department was indeed grieving. He was devastated by what he had done and full of remorse. But neither I nor the police think he killed himself. If he wanted to commit suicide, he would have just added the cyanide directly to his drink."

Again, C.J. was met with wide-eyed stares of shock and disbelief. This drama was a little too English department for her colleagues' tastes.

"Edmund DeBeyer killed Jefferson Daniels. While everyone had the opportunity, he is the only person who had both the capability and desire to kill Jefferson. Edmund DeBeyer placed the cyanide powder in the protein mix before he was killed himself, I would say sometime on the morning he was killed. As a former medical student, he had the skill to make cyanide powder if he didn't want to order it off the internet. Only one person had a motive to kill Jefferson Daniels and that was Edmund. Edmund would never have stood by and allowed someone to take away one of his beloved possessions."

Walter Scovill stood up at the back of the room, his face distorted with anger and contempt. "This is a lovely story, Professor Whitmore, but what proof do you have? I would have thought as a data person, you would have understood that without corroborating evidence this is just cheap talk. Personally, I find the story that *you* are the killer *very* convincing. It is no secret that you despised Edmund. No one saw you collecting your parking meter data at one-fifteen. You say you have data for that time, but you would not be the first academic to make data up. You could have snuck into 40 Knollwood, argued with Edmund, killed him, and gone out again. And, as you have so cleverly pointed out, put poison in Jefferson's protein powder at any time."

Walter smirked at C.J. *This is just the beginning of my revenge, Annie Oakley,* he thought bitterly. From the open door behind him, Walter heard a refined voice.

"I thought it was just my husband who was a self-serving jerk. But it seems to almost be a job requirement around here." Lisa DeBeyer had walked into the seminar room. She was impeccably dressed in an Ann Taylor black suit, and her long strawberry-blond hair was pulled back into a French twist. Despite her brash words, her face was pale with grief.

C.J. gave her a smile.

"Please excuse me for eavesdropping on your meeting. But I was hoping that I would not have to make an appearance. A rather foolish hope, I realize. Why would you accept the only logical explanation offered, when you can search around for another one that is esoteric and unlikely?"

Betsy sighed happily. This day was much more than she could have ever hoped for. It was like actually living an episode of *Law and Order*.

C.J. interjected with a small introduction. "For those of you who haven't met Edmund's widow, this is Lisa DeBeyer. I appreciate her coming today. It isn't easy to talk about very personal details of your life with a group of strangers."

Lisa gave a wry smile. "No, it isn't. But it seems that my life has unsettled all of yours. When C.J. called me last night, I agreed to hover in the background today. I said I would speak up if I thought anyone was stupid enough not to see the obvious truth, despite the corroborating details."

Walter had the decency to blush.

"I can confirm most of the details C.J. shared with you. Jeffie and I were having an affair. I told Edmund about it and our plans to move away a few days before he was killed, and it set in motion what followed." Lisa paused to compose herself. Her tearless, pale blue eyes scanned the crowd. "On the day Edmund was killed, he and Jefferson argued. Edmund told Jefferson he was going to ruin our careers and kill us both. Jefferson killed Edmund to save me. He called me distraught, to tell me about the fight and what he had done. He should have confessed, but we panicked and decided to see if we could get away with it. Instead of doing the right thing, we decided to move away to New Mexico right away and run away from the problem.

"Unfortunately, we weren't quick enough. Edmund had already planted the poison. So it seems we paid the ultimate price for our cowardice." Lisa, now with tears running down her cheeks, stopped speaking.

C.J. gingerly put a hand on Lisa's shoulder and guided her over in the direction of Betsy. This level of grief counseling was beyond C.J.'s skill set.

As her colleagues shifted uncomfortably in their seats, uncertain how to react to this extraordinary tale of love and jealousy that had occurred in their midst, C.J. turned and faced them. "So you see, in the end, there were two lemons. But I think we can agree that one was much more sour than the other."

EPILOGUE

Betsy Williams, caramel whip double latte in hand, eased herself into a couch chair at Wallaby's coffee shop. It was just before eleven, and she knew her friend, C.J. Whitmore, would be arriving any minute. It was a cold morning in mid-November, and the first snow of the season had just started. The arrival of snow never filled Betsy with an intense excitement, the way it did her friends that skied. But it didn't make her sad or depressed either. As far as Betsy was concerned, it was just weather. If you gave it a day or two, it would change.

Truth be told, Betsy had had a hard time getting excited about anything since the murders in the department about two months ago. Since then, everything had seemed a little...well...blah. Some might have described the last few months as calm, or even restful. The routine of Eaton had quickly been restored––classes were taught, research was discussed, and egos were stroked. But to Betsy, her life of teaching and knitting and family potlucks just didn't hold the same thrill it once did.

Betsy turned her head when she heard the familiar clack of cowboy heels approaching. Now, C.J. Whitmore was a woman who seemed to have no trouble adjusting to life post-murder. Despite her heavy teaching load this semester, she had already squeezed in a conference in Banff and was heading to the Bahamas over Thanksgiving break to purportedly discuss the usefulness of Monte Carlo simulations when modeling micro-financial decision points. Or something like that.

"Well, I reckon this is a genuine Goldilocks snowfall," declared C.J. with satisfaction as she sat down next to Betsy, coffee cup in hand. "Not too early, not too late. Probably hit the median start date for the season on the nose."

Betsy smiled, despite herself. C.J. could see data anywhere.

C.J. plunked her feet—and therefore her cowboy boots—up on the coffee table with a comfortable sigh. "Well, I've got news today that would leave a pig open-mouthed at a full trough. You'll never guess who emailed me."

Betsy took a thoughtful sip of coffee. "Is this anything to do with your classes?"

"No," scoffed C.J. "My only thought about teaching right now is 'thank goodness Thanksgiving is only a week away.' You know, just because I solved the murders, it didn't absolve me of having to teach Edmund's class. This semester had been a professional waste of time."

Betsy, who *only* taught classes, didn't comment on this less-than-flattering summary of her life's work. Or the fact that C.J.'s definition of "professional waste of time" was a semester in which she attended not one, but two conferences. Instead, she refocused on the original question. "Did Stephen Choi email you?" she finally asked.

C.J. laughed. "Nope. But I do have news about him, now that you mention it. He posts on Facebook all the time. A real social media hussy...putting out for everyone. Anyway, he's doing great out in Hawaii... never been happier, if you can believe what you read on the internet. You should really get on Facebook, Betsy.

The pics of Stephen in his fireman gear are too cute for words. But that isn't who I was thinking of."

"I don't know about Facebook. I wouldn't know what to write..." Betsy petered out. Maybe she should try Facebook. Her older grandchildren were always talking about it. Besides, what was the worst that could happen? "Well, I might try Facebook. But who are you talking about? Charles? Is he finally retiring?"

C.J. shook her head. "No...wrong again. You know, Charles reminds me of an old horse my father owned. Old Mac—that's the horse—happily sat out in the pasture day after day, and didn't even notice the cars whizzing by on the road next to him. I reckon Charles will be with us, out in the pasture, until he chews his last bite of grass. And that man won't notice the progress that flies right by him while he's here."

Betsy drank some more of her coffee, and looked out the window. "You know, we might get a few inches of snow today."

"Could do, but we aren't changing the topic yet. You really can't guess who I have news about?"

"Well, surely it's too early for Walter to be back."

"Dear Lord yes. And for that I am as thankful as a pig at Hanukkah. Though I can't believe we have to have him back at all. After what he did? And he only had to take a one semester sabbatical at a health farm? The power of tenure. But I'm sure Jose is relieved that he has one semester free of Walter."

Betsy nodded in agreement. She hadn't been surprised that Walter Scovill had escaped any long-term consequences. Eaton closed in around its own. But she had been surprised when Peter Johansson was elected interim Department Chair. Such a mouse of a man. But while the cat's away...

"You still have no idea?"

"None. You'll have to tell me."

"You were just asking about her the other day."

"Her?"

"Uh huh."

"Oh my. You heard from..."

"Yep. Lisa DeBeyer."

"How is she? Where is she?"

"Well, after the police decided not to press any charges, she left New York and went to New Mexico after all."

"Really. To start her art gallery?"

"You'd think so, right? But no. She's...and you aren't going to believe this...this is the show-stopper...she's an alpaca farmer!"

Betsy snorted coffee. "Miss 'Ann Taylor with Manicure'?"

"I know. I can't see it lasting. But you never can tell what crazy something a person will do for someone they love. Even a dead someone."

"Talking of crazy..." said Betsy, her voice trailing off as she looked towards the door where Mary Beth had walked in.

C.J. turned to see Mary Beth dressed in red crocodile-skin pumps, skinny-fit jeans, a t-shirt several sizes too small with a garish "Foster's Beer" logo across her chest, and little stuffed koala earrings dangling from each ear. Closer inspection revealed that her nails had been painted with teeny-tiny kangaroos.

C.J. and Betsy just stared.

"G'day mates!" called Mary Beth, waving over to C.J. and Betsy.

C.J. turned to Betsy. "Well, that's as subtle as a barn cat in heat. I had been enjoying the peace and quiet in the department for the last few months. But I think any tranquility is officially over."

"What on earth has gotten into that girl now?" asked Betsy.

"I can only guess that Mary Beth has seen dear Jeffie's replacement," replied C.J. "The rather attractive and extremely single man from Australia. Poor guy. I hope he survives!"

THE END

ABOUT THE AUTHOR

 J.T. Toman lives in Boulder, Colorado. She received her Ph.D. in economics from Yale University and has taught econometrics at the University of Sydney and the University of Colorado at Boulder. She also has a degree in zookeeping from Pikes Peak Community College and has cared for everything from butterflies to elephants. She now teaches math at Front Range Community College, and truly believes fractions are useful in everyday life.

In her spare time, J.T. Toman joins the rest of Colorado hiking, biking and skiing. However, much like her cats, she finds food more inspiring than scenery. J.T. particularly loves home-grown tomatoes, udon noodles and tall glasses of chocolate milk, though not at the same time.

Picking Lemons is her first novel.